MANCALA MOON

BY

ASA BOWERS

Published by: Asa Bowers
Paperback ISBN: 978-1-7329481-8-1
Hardcover ISBN: 978-1-7329481-9-8
Printed in the United States of America
First Edition, 2026.

CONTENTS

PREFACE

There are no words in any language that can fully capture the journey a soul must take—to feel, to shed, to break, and to begin again.

Yet the attempt itself is sacred.

This is my attempt, and these pages are the result.

Chapter 1:
The Weight of Waking

Three missed calls from the auto shop, two from his landlord, and one from a number he didn't recognize greeted Micah upon waking just slightly after eleven. That last number will have been from his job interview—the one scheduled for ten.

He stared at the cracked ceiling of his studio apartment, the familiar weight of failing at functional adulthood crushing his chest. The apartment held the particular silence of places where hope had quietly expired, a sound Micah found himself achingly intimate with at the tender age of twenty-one. Sunlight filtered through water-spotted windows, catching dust motes that drifted like tiny ghosts through the stale air. He kept the clutter of past-due notices out of the bedroom, storing them instead in the kitchen where he would only occasionally glance at them. But he felt them just the same. Like they put off a vibration that resonated through the floor. Pacific Gas & Electric. Comcast. The medical bill from his last emergency room visit when the panic attacks got too bad.

He should get up. Should charge his phone and call back, apologize, make excuses. Should shower and shave and pretend he was still the kind of person who showed up places on time. Instead, he lay there counting water stains that he should have called the leasing office about. But didn't.

Two years. That's how long it had been since the accident. Since the highway patrol officer stood in his dorm room with that practiced expression of professional sympathy. Since he'd identified what was left of his parents at the county morgue. Two years of everyone telling him he was young, he'd bounce back, these things just took time. As if grief operated on some kind of schedule. As if there was a deadline for learning how to breathe around the hole inside of you.

The insurance money had seemed like so much at first. Not enough to pay his tuition, but college wasn't worth his time anyway. A parade of sneering professors who seemed to wince at the mere sight of him and classmates he couldn't quite be convinced would notice or care if he disappeared one day. He was right about that one. No one had reached out after he'd left campus. Neither had any of his coworkers from the warehouse. He'd quit the job—it was only part time anyway—to take some time, to figure things out. But time had a way of dissolving money like sugar in rain. First the funeral costs, then the months of not working, of barely eating, of letting bills pile up because opening those envelopes felt like lifting mountains. Now he was down to counting quarters for coffee and dodging his landlord in the hallways.

Micah forced himself vertical, bare feet finding the cold linoleum. The studio was maybe four hundred square feet, most of it taken up by a bed that doubled as a couch and a kitchenette that hadn't seen a real meal in weeks. Empty takeout containers formed a small skyline on the counter. Cooking would be cheaper, but he couldn't quite muster up the energy to do it. Even deciding what to order felt like too much some days. The refrigerator hummed its death rattle, a sound he'd grown so accustomed to that silence would probably keep him awake.

He plugged in his phone with the frayed charging cable that only worked if you held it at exactly the right angle. While it struggled back to life, he shuffled to the bathroom. The mirror showed him exactly what he expected: hollow eyes, three days of stubble, hair that couldn't decide which direction to stick up. Twenty-one years old and already wearing his father's expression. That same distant look his dad got after a few beers, staring through the TV at something nobody else could see.

The shower sputtered lukewarm water that smelled faintly of rust. He stood under it until it ran cold, which didn't take long. By the time he got out, his phone had accumulated enough charge to be out of the danger zone. The missed calls reproduced themselves on the lock screen along with seventeen other notifications he didn't have the energy to process. The auto shop had left a voicemail. He played it while pulling on yesterday's jeans.

"Hi Micah, this is Derek from Precision Auto. Just calling about your interview this morning..." The manager's voice carried that particular tone of minor annoyance trying to sound understanding. "Give us a call back if you're still interested in the position."

Still interested. As if interest was the problem. As if he hadn't spent two hours last night researching common interview questions, practicing his answers in the bathroom mirror. Tell us about your biggest weakness. Where do you see yourself in five years? Why do you want to work here?

He'd had all the answers ready. Perfectionism was his weakness, he'd turn it into a strength. Five years, he'd be managing a shop of his own. He wanted to work there because cars were honest. They either ran or they didn't. You could fix what was broken, replace what was worn out. Not like people.

But none of that mattered when you couldn't even wake up on time. When your body felt like it was filled with wet sand and your brain kept shorting out like bad wiring. When the simple act of existing felt like drowning in slow motion.

Micah deleted the voicemail and set the phone aside. Through the thin walls, he could hear his neighbor's TV playing the morning news. Something about the economy, about job growth, about opportunities for young people willing to work hard. The same promises that had been made to his father's generation, and his grandfather's before that. Work hard, pay your dues, and someday you'll have something to show for it. Except his father had worked double shifts at the plant for twenty years and died with nothing but debt and a son who couldn't even hold down a job at a diner.

The coffee maker was empty, had been for days. He found a half-full can of Folgers behind the rice and shook it. Enough for maybe one more pot. Tomorrow's problem. Everything was tomorrow's problem when you could barely handle today.

While the ancient Mr. Coffee wheezed through its cycle, Micah opened his laptop. The screen flickered to life, showing his email inbox. Rejection letters had their own folder now. Thanks for your interest, but we've decided to go with another candidate. Your qualifications are impressive, however… Always however.

He closed the laptop without checking for new messages. Outside, the city went about its business. Cars passed. People with purpose and destinations. People who knew where they were going and why it mattered. Through the window, he could see the bus stop where he used to catch the 47 to work. Sarah would sometimes wait with him there, stealing sips of his coffee, complaining about her morning classes but smiling while she did it.

That was before. Before she started making comments about ambition and self-sabotage and leveling up. She kept saying she'd tried, that last conversation they'd had. She'd *tried*. So hard. Whatever that meant. Yeah, life was hard. But staying was the easiest thing in the world. It was getting up and making changes that was hard. At least for him. But not for Sarah.

The coffee was bitter and burnt, but it was warm. That counted for something. Micah wrapped his hands around the mug and tried to imagine what his next move should be. Call the auto shop back? Update his resume again? Pretend that any of it mattered?

His phone buzzed. A text from a number he didn't recognize. "Hey, saw your resume online. Might have something for you. Call me back." No company name. No details. Probably another pyramid scheme or door-to-door sales job. But he saved the number anyway. When you were drowning, even driftwood looked like a lifeboat.

The morning was already gone. Another day slipping through his fingers like water. Like time. Like everything he couldn't seem to hold onto no matter how tight he gripped. Somewhere in the building, a baby was crying. Somewhere else, a couple was fighting about money. The sounds of other people's lives bleeding through the walls, reminding him that the world kept spinning regardless of whether he participated.

Micah set down the empty mug and pulled out his wallet. Three dollars and forty-seven cents. Enough for bus fare if he needed it. Not enough for much else. Rent was due in five days. The food bank was open on Wednesdays. He'd done the math so many times it had worn grooves in his brain.

He should make a plan. Should do something. Should be something more than this ghost haunting his own life. But the weight was back, pressing down on his chest, making each breath feel like work. This was the part they didn't tell you about grief. Not the crying or the anger or the bargaining with God. The emptiness. The way it carved you hollow and left you echoing.

On the counter, between the unpaid bills and empty containers, sat a photo he couldn't bring himself to put away. His parents at some company picnic, laughing at something outside the frame. His mother's hand on his father's shoulder.

His father looking young and alive and nothing like the man who'd spent his last years staring through television screens at invisible distances.

Micah touched the photo gently, like it might dissolve. Then he turned away. The day was waiting, empty and patient as an open grave. He had nowhere to go and nothing to do when he got there. But sitting still felt like surrender. So he grabbed his jacket, the one with the ripped pocket and the stain he couldn't get out, and headed for the door.

The hallway smelled like cooking oil and industrial cleaner. Someone had taped a notice about a lost cat to the wall. Mr. Whiskers. Orange tabby. Reward if found. Micah wondered if Mr. Whiskers had run away or just wandered off and forgotten how to get home. He wondered if anyone was really looking, or if the signs were just another kind of motion that felt like progress.

Outside, the October air carried the first hints of winter. Not cold yet. California had its perks, even in the Northern half, but cool enough to make him zip his jacket. The street was the same as always. The same cracked sidewalks and graffitied walls. The same broken streetlight the city never seemed to fix. The same sense of being in a place that used to be somewhere and was now just anywhere.

He walked without destination, hands in his pockets, following his feet like they might know something his brain didn't. Past the liquor store where his father used to stop after work. Past the church where his parents had gotten married. Past all the landmarks of a life that felt like it belonged to someone else.

At the corner, he paused. Left would take him toward downtown, toward the auto shop he should call back, toward the possibility of salvaging something from this day. Right led to the park, to the walking paths where he used to run before everything got too heavy to outpace. Straight ahead, the street continued into the kind of neighborhood where people had lawns and futures and children who would grow up believing the world made sense.

Micah stood there, paralyzed by the simple geometry of choice. Three directions. Three possibilities. None of them feeling any more real or important than the others. This was what his life had become. Standing on corners, unable to choose between paths that all led to the same nowhere.

A bus pulled up to the stop, brakes hissing like a tired sigh. The driver looked at him expectantly. Micah shook his head and stepped back. Not yet. Not today. Maybe tomorrow he'd know where he was going. Maybe tomorrow the weight would lift enough to let him care.

The bus pulled away, leaving him alone on the corner. Still three directions. Still nowhere to go. But standing still felt like dying, so he chose left. Toward downtown. Toward the auto shop. Toward the pretense that he was still trying.

One foot in front of the other. That's all it took. That's all it had ever taken. The trick was remembering why it mattered.

The auto shop was closed by the time Micah reached it. "Back in 30 minutes" read the handwritten sign taped to the glass door. He stood there anyway, cupping his hands against the window to peer inside. Tools hung on pegboards like surgical instruments. An old Camaro sat half-dissected on the lift. Everything waiting for someone who knew how to fix what was broken.

He pulled out his phone to call but couldn't make his fingers dial. What was the point? *Sorry I missed the interview. My alarm didn't go off. My life is falling apart. I'm drowning in slow motion and can't seem to remember how to swim.* None of it sounded like something you could say to a stranger who just needed someone reliable to change oil and rotate tires. To watch the shop while the owner went for a prolonged bathroom break.

Instead, he found himself scrolling through social media, that particular form of modern self-torture. His high school friends had scattered like seeds in the wind, taking root in better soil. Marketing jobs in San Francisco. Graduate school in Boston. Teaching English in Japan. Everyone becoming someone while he stood still.

Then David's update appeared, bright and sharp as a knife between the ribs.

"Excited to announce my promotion to Senior Manager! Couldn't have done it without my amazing team and the endless support of my beautiful wife Rachel. God is good! #Blessed #MovingUp"

The photo showed his cousin in a pressed shirt and confident smile, the kind of man who remembered to charge his phone and showed up places on time. David stood in front of a glass office building, morning light making everything gleam like a promise kept. At twenty-five, David owned a house in Walnut Creek. Had a wife who looked at him like he hung the stars. Led a youth group at his church and somehow made it sound fun instead of obligatory.

Micah stared at the photo until his eyes burned. David, who he'd grown up with like brothers after David's mom died. David, who'd lived through the same family gatherings, heard the same stories about their grandfather's drinking and their great-grandfather's "accident" at the factory. David, who'd lost his mother at seven and his father to a heart attack just after graduation, but somehow transformed grief into purpose instead of letting it rot into paralysis.

What was different? What secret ingredient had David found that let him take the same raw materials of loss and build something beautiful instead of this crumbling life?

The comments under David's post were already piling up. "Congratulations!" "So proud of you!" "Well deserved!" Each one a small stone added to the weight on Micah's chest. He knew he should add his own. Should type something supportive and cousin-like. But his thumbs wouldn't move.

A memory surfaced, uninvited. Last Thanksgiving at Aunt Carol's house. David finding him on the back porch, escaping the noise and questions about his plans. They'd stood there watching the neighbor's kids play basketball in the driveway, and David had said, "You know, there's a girl in the church choir that I think you'd like. You should come this week and meet her."

"For what?" Micah had asked, though he knew.

"For something new." David's voice had been gentle, careful.

Micah had made some excuse about work schedules and changed the subject. But he'd seen the look in David's eyes. It wasn't about the girl. Or even church. It was like David could see straight through to the hollow place where faith in anything, even the world itself, was supposed to live and found only empty air.

Now, standing outside the closed auto shop with David's success glowing from his phone screen, Micah wondered if his cousin had been right. If there was some cosmic math where suffering plus faith equaled salvation. If the only difference between them was that David had found something to believe in while Micah had found only the reliability of disappointment.

He closed Facebook and opened his job search app. Fifteen new postings in the area. Warehouse Associate. Customer Service Representative. Delivery Driver. Each listing a variation on the same theme: wanting someone young and eager and undamaged. Someone who could pass a drug test and a background check and show up five days a week without fail. Simple requirements that felt insurmountable when getting out of bed was a daily negotiation.

His phone buzzed. The landlord again. "Rent due Friday. No extensions."

Micah deleted the message and shoved the phone in his pocket. The sun was fighting through the clouds now, making everything look deceptively hopeful. He started walking again, no destination in mind, just movement for the sake of proving he still could.

The pawn shop on Third Street had his father's watch in the window. A Seiko that had survived thirty years of factory work only to end up priced at eighty dollars between someone's wedding ring and a dusty PlayStation. Micah had gotten seventy for it two months ago when the electricity was about to be shut off. The owner had promised to hold it if he wanted to buy it back. But wanting and affording were different countries, and Micah didn't have a passport to cross between them.

He passed the diner where he'd worked until three weeks ago. Through the window, he could see his replacement, some kid who couldn't be more than eighteen, smiling as he refilled coffee cups. The kid moved with the easy confidence of someone who hadn't yet learned how quickly things could shatter. Who still believed that showing up was enough, that hard work guaranteed anything beyond exhaustion.

The manager, Carlos, was behind the register. He looked up as Micah passed, their eyes meeting for a moment through the glass. Carlos raised his hand in what might have been a wave or might have been dismissal. Micah kept walking. There was nothing to say. *Sorry I kept calling in sick. Sorry I couldn't fake the smile anymore. Sorry I made customers uncomfortable with awkward silences and too-long stares.*

His phone buzzed again. This time it was an email. Another rejection, this one from a job he'd forgotten he'd applied for. "After careful consideration, we've decided to pursue other candidates whose qualifications more closely match our needs."

Micah found himself at the library without meaning to go there. It was one of the few places left that didn't require money to exist in. The security guard nodded at him, familiar with his face by now. Inside, the familiar smell of old books and industrial carpet. The quiet that wasn't quite silence, full of whispered conversations and fingers on keyboards and the subtle soundtrack of other people's productivity.

He sat at one of the computers and logged into his email, determined to go through it properly. Inbox zero and all that. Seventeen new messages. Mostly spam. A reminder that his car insurance had lapsed. A notice that his student loans would be coming out of deferment soon. An invitation to join a professional networking site. Each message another thread in the net that kept pulling tighter.

At the next computer, a woman was helping her son with homework. The boy couldn't be more than ten, but he attacked the math problems with determination, tongue poking out in concentration. His mother watched with the patient pride of someone who believed in futures and possibility and the simple equation that effort plus time equaled success.

Micah opened a new browser tab and found himself typing: "How to explain employment gaps."

The results were predictably cheerful. "Turn Your Gap into an Opportunity!" "What Employers Really Want to Know!" "Five Ways to Spin Your Time Off!" Each article assuming that gaps were choices, strategic moves in some grand career chess game.

The woman and her son finished their homework and gathered their things. As they passed, the boy dropped his pencil. Micah picked it up and handed it back. The boy smiled, gap-toothed and grateful. "Thanks, mister."

Such a simple exchange. A pencil dropped, a pencil returned. But it left Micah feeling oddly hollow, as if even that small interaction had taken more than he had to give.

He sat there until the librarian announced they'd be closing in fifteen minutes. Then he logged off and walked back out into the fading afternoon light. The day was almost over. Another one crossed off whatever calendar was keeping track. Another day survived, if survival was the right word for this careful navigation between one empty moment and the next.

His phone had one new notification. David had tagged him in the promotion post. "Thanks cuz! Couldn't have made it through those tough early years without family. Love you man."

The words blurred as Micah stared at them. Family. Love. The casual assumption that they were still connected by more than just shared DNA and divergent paths. He knew he should respond. Should like the post at minimum. Should perform the small social ritual that maintained the fiction they were still close.

Instead, he turned off his phone and started the long walk back to his apartment. The streets were filling with commuters heading home from real jobs to real lives. People with answers to the question "What do you do?" People who knew where they'd be tomorrow and next week and five years from now.

The weight settled heavier as he walked. Not just on his chest now, but in his legs, his arms, the space behind his eyes.

This was what the men in his family carried. This was the inheritance passed down through generations like a cursed heirloom no one knew how to refuse.

By the time he reached his building, the sun was setting, painting the sky in shades of amber and ash. Beautiful and terrible, like everything else. Like the whole world offering its gifts to people who knew how to receive them while he stood outside, hands full of nothing, wondering why he'd been built without whatever let others open their arms and accept.

****

Micah heated a can of soup on the stove, the kind that tasted more like salt than anything else, and ate standing at the counter. He needed to do laundry. Needed to wash the dishes piling in the sink. Needed to do a hundred small things that constituted a normal life. Instead, he found himself at the closet, pulling down the cardboard box he'd been avoiding for months.

His mother's handwriting on the side: "Family Photos & Documents." She'd been the keeper of histories, the one who made sure someone remembered birthdays and anniversaries and the names of cousins twice removed. After the accident, the hospital had given him her purse, her wallet, the wedding ring they'd had to cut off. Small artifacts of a life interrupted. But this box—this was what she'd thought worth preserving.

Micah set it on the bed and lifted the lid. The smell of old paper and his mother's perfume, faint but unmistakable. On top, loose photographs. His parents' wedding. His first day of kindergarten. Family barbecues where everyone still smiled like they meant it.

Beneath the photos, manila folders labeled in his mother's careful script. "Insurance." "Medical Records." "Family History." He pulled out the last one, not sure what he was looking for but feeling the pull of it anyway.

Inside, older documents. His grandfather's death certificate. Korea, 1952. Twenty-eight years old. His grandmother's obituary, ten years later. "Died peacefully at home," which Micah knew meant she'd drunk herself to death in the bedroom while his father watched cartoons in the next room.

Deeper in the folder, a photocopy of something older. His great-grandfather's accident report from the Portland Steel Works. 1951. Crushed by machinery on the factory floor. Thirty-four years old. Left behind a wife and three children. The report was clinical, matter-of-fact. Machine operator error. No safety violations found. As if dying at thirty-four was just another workplace hazard.

Micah spread the documents across his bed like tarot cards. His father, thirty-nine. His grandfather, twenty-eight. His great-grandfather, thirty-four. Young men who should have had decades ahead of them, cut down in their prime. A pattern too consistent to be coincidence.

But that wasn't the worst part. The worst part was what he found next.

A family tree his mother had been working on, penciled notes in the margins. She'd traced the family line back five generations, and there it was, clear as a diagnosis. Every male in his direct line dead before forty. His great-great-grandfather, drowning. Thirty-six. His great-great-great-grandfather, tuberculosis. Twenty-nine. As far back as she'd searched, the same story. Young death. Widows left behind. Sons growing up to repeat the pattern.

Except David.

Micah found the branch where their family lines diverged. David's father had been his father's first cousin; their grandfathers were brothers. Same blood. Same history. But David's line showed a different pattern. His grandfather had lived to seventy-two. His father had made it to sixty-eight before the heart attack. Not young men claimed by mysterious accidents or sudden illness. Just ordinary death at ordinary ages.

What was different? What protected David's branch while Micah's withered on the vine?

He dug deeper into the box, finding letters, newspaper clippings, fragments of family lore. A letter from his great-grandmother to her sister: "The men in this family are cursed, I swear it. Like something's hunting them through the years."

A newspaper clipping from 1962: "Local Man Dies in Fishing Accident." His great-uncle, his grandfather's brother. Thirty-three years old.

Another clipping, older, edges crumbling: "Factory Worker Found Dead." No date, but the man's name was familiar from the family tree. Another ancestor, another early grave.

Micah's hands shook as he sorted through the evidence. Not that he needed it. The nothingness waiting for him in life had always been apparent. It was almost vindicating to see it laid out in black and white, assuming he still had the capacity to feel such an emotion.

In the bottom of the folder, he found something that made his breath catch. A photograph, old enough that the edges had yellowed. A young man who could have been Micah's twin standing in front of a forest. Dense trees, shadows between them dark as spilled ink. On the back, in faded pencil: "Theodore. 1897."

Theodore. Micah found him on the family tree. His great-great-great uncle. Disappeared at age twenty-four, body never found. Presumed dead. The photograph showed him smiling, unaware of whatever waited in those woods. Or maybe he did know. Maybe that's why he was smiling. Maybe he was tired of running from something that would catch him anyway.

Micah held the photograph up to the lamp. The forest behind Theodore seemed to shift in the unsteady light, shadows moving between the trees like living things. It was just an old photo, damaged by time and handling. But something about it made his skin crawl. Something about the way Theodore stood at the very edge of the frame, as if he was about to step backward into those waiting shadows and never emerge.

A knock at the door made him jump. Mrs. Chen from upstairs, probably. She sometimes brought him leftovers, worried about the thin young man who never seemed to eat. But when he opened the door, no one was there. Just the empty hallway and the flickering fluorescent light that maintenance never fixed.

He closed the door and returned to the bed. The soup he'd eaten sat heavy in his stomach. Outside, a siren wailed, racing toward someone else's emergency. Inside, the silence felt thick, expectant, like the moment before a storm breaks.

Micah gathered the documents with shaking hands. His mother had known. She'd mapped out the pattern, traced the curse or whatever it was through the generations. Is that why she'd always looked at him with such sadness? Not just maternal worry, but the specific grief of someone who could see the future written in the past?

He found one last item in the box. A small leather journal, water-stained and worn. Inside, his mother's writing, but younger, more hurried. Entries from when his father was still alive.

"Michael came home late again. Won't say where he's been. That distant look is back, the one his father had. The one they all get before—"

The entry cut off mid-sentence.

Another entry, dated a month later: "Found Michael in the garage, just sitting in the car with the engine off. Said he was thinking. About what? Won't tell me. I'm scared. The pattern is so clear. Why can't he see it? Why can't any of them see it?"

The final entry, a week before the accident: "Michael says I worry too much. Says there's no such thing as curses. But I've done the research. I've traced it back. Something happened. Something our family did or didn't do. And now the men pay for it, generation after generation. I won't let it take him. I won't let it take our son."

But it had taken his father anyway. A rainy night. A tired truck driver. A physics equation that ended with two people dead and one son left to carry whatever weight had been passed down through all those shortened lives.

Micah closed the journal and set it aside. His hands weren't shaking anymore. Instead, he felt oddly calm, the way hypothermia victims supposedly felt warm just before the end. Here was proof of what he'd always suspected. He wasn't just depressed or unlucky or failing at life. He was marked. Claimed by something that had been patient enough to wait through generations but always collected its due.

Micah turned off the light and lay back on the bed, surrounded by the paper remnants of abbreviated lives. In the darkness, he could almost feel them. All those young men who'd died too soon. All those fathers who'd never seen their sons grow up. All those sons who'd grown up to repeat the pattern.

Tomorrow he would put the documents away. Tomorrow he would call the auto shop and try to salvage something from the missed interview. Tomorrow he would pretend that knowing about the pattern didn't change everything.

But tonight, he lay in the dark and wondered if Theodore had felt this same weight before he walked into those woods and never came back. If all the men in his family had eventually reached this moment of recognition. This understanding that they weren't just living their own lives but carrying forward some terrible inheritance that would claim them no matter how hard they ran.

Outside, the city went on with its business of living. Inside, Micah lay still as a corpse, practicing for what felt inevitable, surrounded by the paper ghosts of all the men who'd practiced before him and gotten it right.

Sleep came like drowning, slow and then all at once.

Micah had dozed off without meaning to, still fully dressed, the family documents scattered across the bedspread like leaves after a storm. The afternoon had dissolved into evening while he lay there, paralyzed by the weight of inherited doom. Now the apartment was full dark, only the streetlight outside casting thin bars of amber through the blinds.

In that liminal space between waking and sleeping, the familiar sounds of the building—pipes groaning, footsteps overhead, the distant murmur of television—began to fade. They were replaced by something else. Wind through branches. The rustle of leaves. The particular silence of deep woods where civilization's constant hum couldn't reach.

Then he was there.

The forest rose around him, ancient and immediate. Not the scraggly urban trees he knew from city parks, but old growth that had never known an axe. Trunks thick as houses soared toward a canopy so dense it turned day to twilight. The air smelled of earth and moss and that green scent of things growing in shadow.

Micah stood on a path that might have been deer trail or might have been older, worn by feet that walked here before California had a name. He was wearing the same clothes he'd fallen asleep in, but they felt different here. Lighter. As if the weight he carried in the waking world couldn't follow him into dream.

"You came."

He turned to find his father standing between two massive oaks. Not the father from the morgue, face reconstructed by morticians who'd done their best with what the accident left them. This was his father from before—whole, solid, wearing the flannel shirt Micah had given him their last Christmas together.

"Dad?" The word came out younger than Micah's voice had been in years.

His father smiled, that crooked expression that appeared so rarely in life. Behind him, another figure emerged from the shadows. Micah's grandfather, looking exactly like the photos from Korea but without the thousand-yard stare. He wore his uniform, but it was clean, unbloodied, as if war had never touched it.

"About time," his grandfather said. His voice was rougher than his son's, carved by cigarettes and whatever he'd seen in the jungle. "We've been waiting."

"Waiting for what?"

But they were already turning, walking deeper into the forest. Micah followed without choosing to, his feet finding their own way along the path. The trees seemed to lean in as he passed, as if they'd been expecting him too.

They walked in silence, three generations of broken men made whole by the silent laws of dreams. The path wound between roots thick as anacondas, past streams that caught light that shouldn't exist beneath such dense canopy. Time moved strangely. They might have walked for minutes or hours, the forest unchanging around them, always ancient, always just beginning.

Then the trees opened into a clearing.

In the center stood a sign, weathered wood on a post that looked like it had grown from the ground rather than been planted. The words were carved deep, in a language Micah didn't recognize but somehow understood:

"All who enter feed the forest.

All who feed the forest enter.

The door closes behind but never ahead."

His father and grandfather stood on either side of the sign, waiting. Beyond it, the path continued into shadows so thick they looked solid.

The wind picked up, moving through the canopy with a sound like whispered names. Micah heard his own among them, carried on the breeze like a question. The forest was asking. Inviting. Promising something he couldn't quite grasp.

But the dream was shifting. His father and grandfather were fading, becoming translucent as the forest grew more solid around them. The sign remained, its carved words pulsing with a light that hurt to look at directly.

"Wait," Micah called, but they were already gone. He stood alone in the clearing, the sign before him, the path beyond beckoning.

He took a step forward.

The moment his foot crossed the threshold where the sign stood, the forest changed. The trees were the same but different, older, hungrier. The air grew thick, almost liquid.

And from somewhere deeper in the woods, something called his name. Not with words but with a pull he felt in his bones, in his blood, in the hollow places where hope used to live.

He wanted to follow that call more than he'd wanted anything in two years. More than he'd wanted to save his parents. More than he'd wanted Sarah to stay. More than he'd wanted to wake up tomorrow and feel like living was worth the effort.

Another step. Another. The forest welcomed him, branches parting like curtains. This was what his father had felt. His grandfather. Theodore with his knowing smile. This was why they'd died young—not from curse but from calling. They'd heard the forest's invitation and said yes, one way or another.

"Micah."

A different voice. Familiar but out of place. David's voice, coming from behind him.

He turned. His cousin stood at the edge of the clearing, but he looked wrong. Too bright. Like someone had cut him out of a different picture and pasted him into this one. Light clung to him, not forest light but something else. Something that made the shadows draw back.

They stood there, cousins separated by more than the clearing. Two branches of the same tree, growing toward different light. Micah felt the pull of the forest, patient and eternal. David carried his own gravity, bright and foreign to this place.

The forest began to dissolve, trees becoming walls, moonlight becoming streetlight through blinds. But the feeling remained. The calling. The certainty that somewhere out there, a forest waited with his name carved into its shadows.

Micah woke gasping, heart hammering against his ribs. The room was exactly as he'd left it, family documents still spread across the bed, the photograph of Theodore face-up on the pillow. But everything felt different. Charged. As if the dream had left some residue on the waking world.

He sat up, throat dry as sand. The clock read 3:47 AM, that haunted hour when the body's defenses were lowest. The dream clung to him like smoke. He could still smell the forest, earthy and green and alive. Could still feel the pull of whatever waited beyond that sign. Could still hear his name carried on wind that didn't exist.

Micah gathered the family documents with trembling hands, shoving them back into the box. But he kept Theodore's photograph, studying it in the weak light. The forest behind his ancestor looked different now. Familiar. Like somewhere he'd been rather than somewhere he'd seen.

He went to his laptop and opened a search engine, fingers moving without conscious thought. He typed: "Ancient forest California missing persons warning sign."

The results were immediate and numerous. Forums, news articles, blogs dedicated to urban legends and unexplained disappearances. He clicked through them, speed-reading, looking for something specific without knowing what.

Then he found it.

A photograph on someone's hiking blog, posted three years ago. "Creepiest thing I've ever seen on a trail. This sign in the middle of nowhere. Gave me such bad vibes I turned around immediately."

The image was slightly blurry, taken in haste, but the sign was unmistakable. The same weathered wood. The same carved words, though in the photograph they were in English:

"All who enter feed the forest.

All who feed the forest enter.

The door closes behind but never ahead."

Below the photo, comments warned others to stay away. Stories of hikers who'd ventured past the sign and come back changed, speaking of shadows that moved wrong and paths that led in circles. Others who'd never come back at all.

Micah found the location tagged in the post. The Mendocino National Forest, six hours north. Remote, mostly undeveloped, the kind of place where you could walk for days without seeing another person. The kind of place where someone could disappear and never be missed.

He bookmarked the page, then found himself searching for more. Every result led to another, a rabbit hole of similar stories. The forest appeared in local folklore going back generations. Native stories about a place where the veil was thin. Pioneer accounts of settlers who'd wandered in and come out decades later, unchanged, speaking of impossible things. Modern disappearances blamed on everything from serial killers to Sasquatch.

But through all the stories ran a common thread. The forest called certain people. Not everyone—most hikers passed through unaware of anything unusual. But some heard their names on the wind. Some dreamed of paths between ancient trees. Some felt a pull they couldn't explain, drawing them back again and again until one day they didn't return.

People like Theodore. Like the men in his family, drawn by something older than memory.

Micah closed the laptop as dawn light began seeping through the blinds. He should sleep. Should eat something. Should do any of the normal, healthy things that constituted taking care of himself.

Instead, he pulled up Google Maps on his phone, calculating distances. Six hours by car, assuming he could afford the gas. Eight by bus, with transfers. Possible to do in a day if he left early. Just to see. Just to prove to himself that it was only a forest, only a sign, only his depression manifesting as mystical thinking.

But even as he thought it, he knew better. The dream hadn't felt like symbolism or psychology. It had felt like memory. Like something in his blood recognizing its home.

He looked at the family documents scattered on his bed. All those early deaths. All those young men claimed before their time. Maybe they hadn't been running from something. Maybe they'd been running toward it.

The calling.

Micah set down his phone and went to the window, looking out at the city coming awake. Delivery trucks rumbling past. Early commuters heading to real jobs and real lives. The ordinary world doing its ordinary business.

But overlaid on it now, transparent as a ghost, he could see the forest. Could feel it out there, waiting. Patient as stone.

CHAPTER 2:
DIGITAL DESCENT

The blue glow of Micah's laptop splashed across his face, making him look ghoulish in the window reflection. Three in the morning had become his most productive hour, when the world fell quiet enough that he could pretend his life was unfolding exactly as it should. Tonight felt different though. Tonight he had purpose.

His fingers found the keyboard with an energy he hadn't felt in months. The dream clung to him like cobwebs, guiding his search: *ancient forest Northern California, warning signs old growth redwoods, missing hikers Humboldt County*. It had been so long since he'd been motivated like this, something he took a moment to be disgusted with himself about. But the dreams couldn't be ignored.

Especially now. Looking at his computer screen, at what his search had produced… the photographs stopped him cold.

Coast redwoods rose like cathedral pillars into mist, their trunks so massive they seemed to belong to an older world. Shafts of golden light speared through the canopy, illuminating carpets of ferns that looked soft as velvet. In one image, a trail wound between giants whose tops vanished into fog, creating a natural corridor that seemed to lead somewhere beyond the merely physical. This is what he had seen. The trees weren't similar. This was identical. He had been in *this* particular forest in his sleep.

How was that even possible?

He saved every image, screenshot every trail map. His coffee grew cold as he built a digital shrine to this place he'd never seen but somehow recognized. The forest had a dozen names depending on who was talking: Whispering Pines to the locals, Shadow Grove in older documents, and in one academic paper about Native American place names, something that translated roughly to "Where the Veil Grows Thin."

The browser tabs multiplied like an infection. A hiking blog from 2018 described "atmospheric anomalies" in the deep groves. A paranormal investigation site claimed electronic devices failed predictably past certain markers. Even the pragmatic reviews on AllTrails carried an undercurrent of unease: *Beautiful but stick to marked trails. Seriously. My GPS went haywire and I lost four hours I can't account for.*

Micah's notebook filled with coordinates, elevations, trail names. The repetition across sources was what made his hand pause mid-sentence. Different decades, different writers, but the same details surfaced like bones through soil. The sense of being watched. Paths that seemed to shift when you weren't looking. Voices that sounded familiar calling from directions that didn't exist.

A Reddit post from six months ago made him lean closer to the screen:

My dad died there. At least I think he did. They never found him. I've been dreaming about him and I don't know what to do. It's been three years, but I still think about it every day. Maybe I should go visit that place.

The username was throwaway_forest_dreams. No posts after that one. No updates. No resolution.

Micah copied the text, hands trembling slightly. The parallels were too precise for comfort. He clicked through to the user's profile, hoping for something more, but found only that single cry for help echoing in the digital void.

The park service website was more clinical but no less disturbing. Seventeen people reported missing in the greater area over the last decade. Most were found within 72 hours, disoriented but unharmed. But several remained unaccounted for, their photos lined up like a gallery of the lost: Marcus Chen, 24, Berkeley engineering student. Rebecca Martinez, 32, single mother from Fresno. Thomas Wright, 29, veteran. Sean Stone, 26, poet and bartender.

All young. All carrying something heavy in their eyes even in the casual photos their families had provided. Micah recognized that weight. He saw it every morning in his bathroom mirror.

By four-thirty, he'd traced the forest's location to a section of Humboldt County accessible only by a series of increasingly sketchy roads. The kind of place where cell service died long before you reached the trailhead. Where help, if you needed it, was hours away through terrain that didn't forgive mistakes.

His notebook had filled three pages now, his handwriting getting smaller and more urgent with each discovery. He'd mapped the disappearances by date, looking for patterns. Spring and fall seemed particularly active. Times of transition, when the world itself felt uncertain about which season it belonged to.

The fog was apparently legendary. Locals called it the "Redwood Veil," a mist that could roll in without warning and turn midday into twilight. Park rangers had protocols for when it descended: stay put, blow your whistle every thirty seconds, wait for it to pass. But the missing persons reports suggested not everyone followed protocol. Or maybe the fog didn't always follow the rules either.

He found a scanned newspaper article from 1987, the photo quality degraded but the headline clear: *UC Davis Student Vanishes in Redwood Wilderness.* The details were frustratingly sparse. James Morrison had told friends he needed to "clear his head" after a bad breakup. His car was found at the trailhead three days later, keys in the ignition, camping gear untouched in the trunk, as if he'd meant to just take a quick walk and come right back.

Thirty-six years ago, but the pattern held. Young person in crisis, drawn to the forest, swallowed by something that left no trace except absence. Every missing person felt like a description of him, like someone who would have been his friend.

Assuming he'd ever had one of those as an adult.

As dawn crept toward his window, he finally pushed back from the laptop. His neck ached and his mouth tasted like stale coffee, but his mind hummed with purpose. The forest existed. It was real, mappable, reachable by car. It had a history of calling to people like him and keeping them.

A stab of jealousy ripped through him. *Where did that come from? Going missing in a forest isn't like getting chosen for a game show, for goodness sake!*

He picked up a pen to add one final note to his research, then stopped. His handwriting from hours ago looked steady, determined. But now the pen shook in his grip, and he realized what he'd spent the night doing.

He'd been planning his own disappearance.

The thought should have frightened him more than it did. But as he looked around his barren apartment, at the overdue bills and empty refrigerator and all the evidence of a life that had never quite started, he felt only relief.

He closed his laptop and stumbled toward bed, exhausted but too wired to sleep. Tomorrow he'd start planning the practical details. Map the route, calculate gas money, figure out what supplies a person carried into a forest that might not let them leave. But for now, he lay in the growing light and let his mind drift back to those photographs.

Ancient trees holding up the sky. Mist that moved like something alive. Paths that led deeper than any map could follow.

Somewhere, the forest waited. And for the first time since his parents' funeral, since Sarah's goodbye, since everything fell apart, Micah felt like he was exactly where he needed to be.

Sleep eluded him until noon, and when he finally woke, the pull was stronger. Micah made instant coffee with shaking hands and returned to his laptop like an addict to a fix. Thanks to his late night of internet scavenging, he had names to follow. Real people who'd walked the path he was contemplating.

Each case of the disappeared was intriguing. The dates scattered across decades but the pattern held firm: dreams that colonized waking life, dead loved ones as guides, an overwhelming sense of being called "home" to a place they'd never been.

But it was the survivors' accounts that truly shook him.

Buried in the comments section of a 2016 blog post about the disappearances, he found someone claiming to have returned from Shadow Grove after twelve days missing. The username was GreenManWalking, and his story read like a fever dream:

"Time doesn't work right in the deep groves. I'd check my watch and hours would pass between seconds, or seconds would stretch into days. The missing people are there, but they're not missing, if that makes sense. They've found what they came for. I saw my brother (car accident, 2009) building something out of fog and light. He looked at me like I was the ghost."

When pressed for why he came back, GreenManWalking's response was simple: *"I didn't come back. I just kept walking and then I was back at the parking lot. It was like the place spit me out and everything was normal again."*

Another account, posted on a paranormal forum in 2019, described a woman who'd entered the forest after her miscarriage and emerged three days later, though she insisted she'd only been gone for a few hours. *"I can't explain what I saw, but I wasn't afraid. It was like being inside a living cathedral. Everything that hurt in the real world just... didn't. I only left because I remembered my sister was picking me up from the airport. Such a stupid, ordinary thing, but it pulled me back like a rope."*

The phrase appeared again and again in survivor accounts: "pulled back." Always by some small obligation, some thread of connection to the ordinary world. A job interview. A pet needing feeding. A library book due for return. The forest, it seemed, released those who still had anchors in consensus reality.

Micah looked around his apartment. No pets. No plants that weren't already dead. No job expecting him. His phone hadn't rung for anything but collections calls and the request for an interview that somehow he couldn't make himself follow up on.

He felt his eyes pulled back to the photographs on the screen again, this time focusing on the beauty rather than the danger. The coast redwoods were among the oldest living things on Earth, some born before Rome fell. They created their own weather systems, harvesting moisture from fog to survive droughts that would kill lesser trees. Their groves were ecosystems unto themselves, vertical worlds where life existed at every level from forest floor to crown.

There was so much lore about old forests in Europe; but somehow the millennia-old Redwoods managed to keep their secrets. Or maybe the natives who knew had all died with their knowing, leaving the next generations to stumble blindly.

In one photograph, morning light transformed mist into golden veils between the trees. Another showed a fairy ring, where redwoods grew in a perfect circle around the phantom of their dead parent tree.

Like a fairy circle, but bigger. More majestic.

Noon crept through his windows as his mind drifted back to Mom's memories. She'd been focused on the litany of early deaths that plagued the men. Of course that made sense. Their deaths foretold the future of her husband and son. But for now, Micah was very much alive. And he wondered what his family did while they still lived. Before they died too soon.

Mom had done the heavy lifting on a popular genealogy site, but he'd never looked at it. Looking back never interested him. Neither did looking forward. It was only about the here and now—the miserable unending *now*. Maybe that was part of the problem. Maybe that was why evaporating into a forest sounded so appealing.

Logging on to the site, he started with what he knew: his father Michael, dead at thirty-nine. Grandfather James, dead at twenty-eight in Korea. Great-grandfather Harold, dead at thirty-four. The pattern was so consistent it might have been scripted. But it wasn't just death that marked his family line. As he dug deeper, a different pattern emerged—one that made him push back from the screen.

Wait… do I come from a family of criminals?

Staring back at him from the screen was a long list of relatives and their malfeasance. Maybe there was a logical explanation for all the early deaths. And it was equally logical why Mom never brought any of this up at the dinner table.

The newspaper archive from 1923 told the story in fading typeface: *"Local Church Treasurer Flees with Building Fund."* Harold Thorne, his great-grandfather, had embezzled three thousand dollars from First Methodist of Framingham—a fortune in those days. The family had fled Massachusetts in disgrace, heading west like so many American scandals before them.

But Harold wasn't the first. Micah traced the line backward, finding a trail of religious disasters that read like a generational curse. Harold's father, William, had been excommunicated from his congregation in 1891 for adultery with the minister's daughter. Before that, Josiah Thorne had been prosecuted in 1856 for posing as a traveling preacher and defrauding three congregations across Connecticut.

Each generation trying to grasp God and coming away with burned fingers.

The family identified as Christian—Micah could see that in census records, marriage certificates, the occasional baptismal record. But it was Christianity held at arm's length, like handling something radioactive. They claimed the label but never the practice. Churches attended briefly, then abandoned. Bibles owned but never opened. Faith professed but never lived.

His father had been the same. Micah remembered finding the massive family bible in his dad's storage unit after the funeral, pages worn with age, but entirely unmarked. It had gone with the rest of it to the liquidation sale.

A scanned letter from 1924 made him stop scrolling. Written by his great-grandmother to her sister back east:

"Harold says the curse followed us from Massachusetts. He speaks wildly sometimes about God turning His face from our line, about sins that compound interest. I tell him it's the guilt talking, that forgiveness is always possible. But then I see how David's cousins prosper while our men wither, and I wonder if some families are marked from the beginning."

David's cousins. Even then, the comparison burned.

He thought about the missing people in Shadow Grove, drawn by dreams and voices. About his father's empty Bible and his grandfather's desperate prayers in Korea that went unanswered. About great-grandfather Harold stealing from God's house and running west, always west, as if geography could outdistance judgment.

But they'd ended up here, in the shadow of ancient forests where older things than Christianity waited. Things that didn't care about baptism or salvation or the Protestant work ethic. Things that measured debt in different currencies.

A memory surfaced: his father taking him to church exactly once, when Micah was seven. Easter Sunday. They'd sat in the back row, his father sweating in an ill-fitting suit, fidgeting like something was crawling on his skin. Halfway through the sermon, his father had grabbed his hand and they'd left, quickly, quietly, like thieves escaping a scene. In the parking lot, his father had muttered, "It's not for us, son. It's never been for us."

Now Micah understood. Some families built churches. Some families robbed them.

No wonder Mom never brought it up at dinner.

His family carried some kind of spiritual poison that turned faith rancid in their hands. David's line had escaped it somehow, had found or maintained some protection that let them walk freely where Micah's ancestors stumbled and fell.

Micah saved his research and rubbed his eyes. Three in the morning again, the hour when insomniacs and the haunted compared notes across the digital void. His family history sprawled across browser tabs like evidence of a crime he hadn't committed but would somehow pay for.

No wonder the forest called to him. It promised something his bloodline had never been able to find in churches: an ending. Whether salvation or damnation, at least it would be final.

Sleep came for him at dawn, pulling him under with hands made of mist and memory. The forest was waiting, but this time it had grown. Fed by his research, nourished by the photographs he'd studied until his eyes burned, the dream forest had become a world unto itself.

He stood barefoot on a carpet of redwood needles that released their sharp green scent with each step. The trees rose around him like the pillars of a cathedral built before humans knew what cathedrals were. Their trunks disappeared into mist that moved with purpose, coiling between the ancient columns like something alive.

This wasn't the generic forest of his earlier dreams. This was Shadow Grove. He recognized specific trees from photographs: the hollow giant that hikers could stand inside, the fairy ring where new growth surrounded the ghost of a parent tree, the grove where Marcus Chen's backpack had been found, contents arranged like an offering.

His father stood in a shaft of golden light that fell through the canopy, looking younger than Micah ever remembered seeing him, the worry lines smoothed away, the perpetual tension gone from his shoulders.

Behind him, others emerged from the mist. Micah recognized them from his research—the missing given form and flesh. Marcus Chen still wore his Berkeley hoodie, but it seemed woven from fog now. Rebecca Martinez carried her daughter's photograph, but the image shifted and lived within the frame. Thomas Wright stood at attention in fatigues that flickered between desert tan and forest green, as if he existed in two wars at once.

The path beneath his feet was soft with centuries of fallen needles, but as he walked deeper, following his father's translucent form, he began to notice things that didn't belong in any photograph. Carvings in the bark that looked like text but hurt to read directly. Shadows that fell upward. Places where the air itself seemed edited, reality's grammar broken and reformed.

He woke gasping, sheets soaked with sweat that smelled of redwood bark and old earth. Dawn light slanted through his window, pale and unconvincing after the forest's eternal twilight. His hands shook as he reached for his notebook, needing to record the dream before it faded.

But when he looked at his palms, the shaking stopped.

Dirt clung to the lifelines. Where had that come from? Had he grabbed something dirty before he fell asleep?

Micah closed his closed laptop.

Tomorrow. I'll go tomorrow.

But his body was already leaning toward the door, toward his car keys, toward the forest that grew more real with each dream. For him, everything was always to be done later or tomorrow. But this time, his body rebelled against the procrastination, refusing to listen to the hesitancy that had kept him inert all this time.

Tomorrow was too far away. The forest was calling now, in broad daylight, in voices that sounded like wind and blood and home.

Micah picked up his car keys, then forced himself to sit, to breathe, to think practically even as the dream whispered to him. If he was going to do this, he would do it right.

His bank account held $247.63. The math was merciless: sixty dollars for gas, maybe seventy with current prices. That left just enough for basic supplies if he was careful, if he didn't pretend this was a normal camping trip requiring normal equipment.

He made a list on the back of his final paycheck stub:

- Sleeping bag (Dad's, in the storage unit)

- Flashlight (batteries?)

- Water bottles

- Granola bars

- Matches/lighter

- Phone charger (pointless, but habit)

- Notebook and pen

The storage unit was a twenty-minute walk that felt like crossing between worlds. He'd been so aimless, so stuck for so long, that moving with purpose made his muscles ache and his breath catch. Like he was running a marathon instead of taking a walk.

The lock was rusty, fighting him as if it knew what he'd come for. Inside, boxes towered like abandoned buildings, each one a testament to his parents' interrupted life—the things he couldn't bear to sell off. He found the camping gear in the back, his father's Coleman sleeping bag that smelled of smoke from fires never lit, promises never kept.

At the bottom of the bag, wrapped in plastic: his grandfather's compass. The brass was tarnished but the needle still pointed true, quivering eagerly like a dog catching a scent. Micah pocketed it, though he suspected it would point toward Shadow Grove no matter which way he turned it.

Back at his apartment, he laid out his supplies like a ritual. The Coleman bag unrolled on his floor, revealing mouse holes and memories. The flashlight with batteries that would last maybe ten hours. Three water bottles from under his sink. A box of granola bars from the back of his cupboard, past their expiration but still sealed.

He should tell someone where he was going. The thought passed through his mind like smoke. Tell who? David, who would probably drive over immediately and ask him to come to church with him? His landlord, who just wanted next month's rent? There was no one in his life who would notice his absence for days, maybe weeks.

The realization should have depressed him. Instead, it felt like freedom. Clean. No loose threads to tangle his departure.

He opened Google Maps one more time, memorizing the route in case the signal cut out. Highway 101 North to 299 East, then a series of increasingly minor roads until asphalt gave way to gravel, gave way to dirt. The satellite view showed green so dense it looked black, an ocean of trees with no safe harbors.

Shadow Grove itself wasn't marked, but he'd triangulated its location from missing person reports and old trail maps. A blank spot on modern charts where cartographers' instruments failed and satellites saw only static.

Micah packed everything into his father's backpack, another relic that had been waiting in storage for this moment. The weight felt right on his shoulders, like inheritance should feel. Heavy but bearable. A burden that had always been his to carry.

He wrote his passwords on a sticky note, left it on his laptop. Took out the trash. Watered the dead plant out of some reflexive courtesy to life, however failed. These small acts of closure felt like preparing a corpse for viewing. Making things tidy for whoever came after.

The apartment key went under the mat where the landlord would find it eventually. No note. What would he say? "Not sure if I'll be back, please don't throw out my stuff… yet." The truth was too complicated for paper.

Micah loaded his supplies into the car, each movement deliberate and final. He'd made this choice in increments— each nightmare, each hour of research, each discovered connection drawing him closer to this moment. But now, with his hand on the car door, the full weight of it settled on him.

He was driving toward his own disappearance. Knowingly. Willingly.

What exactly was he hoping for?

He didn't exactly know. Or care. But there was an insistence roiling within him that whatever he found would be what he needed.

The engine turned over on the first try, eager as everything else seemed to be.

He pulled out of the parking lot without looking back. In the rearview mirror, his apartment building shrank and vanished, already as insubstantial as a dream. The real world—whatever that meant—was ahead of him now.

CHAPTER 3:
CROSSING THE THRESHOLD

The old Honda's heater struggling against an unusual cold that seemed to have settled over the highway, the gas station coffee growing bitter in the cup holder beside him.

His hands gripped the steering wheel tighter than necessary. The farther north he drove, the more the landscape began to change—urban sprawl giving way to farmland, then rolling hills, then the first hints of real forest. Around Ukiah, the trees started crowding closer to the highway, their shadows deep even in the growing light.

The GPS flickered on the dashboard, seeming to struggle with the satellite connection, despite being on a state highway.

"Recalculating," the mechanical voice announced for the fourth time in ten minutes.

He reached over to tap the screen, and for a moment, the map showed him surrounded by green—no roads at all, just an endless expanse of forest. Then it snapped back to normal. Highway 101. Sixty-three miles to his destination.

The pull had been growing stronger since he'd crossed the Golden Gate. At a rest stop near Cloverdale, he'd dozed for twenty minutes and dreamed of walking between trees so massive they made him feel like an insect. He'd woken with the taste of evergreen on his tongue.

Now, as the sun climbed higher, painting the hills gold, Micah found himself checking the rearview mirror more often. Not because anyone was following him—the highway was nearly empty—but because each time he looked back, the road seemed less substantial than the one ahead. As if the world he was leaving was already beginning to fade.

His phone, propped in its holder, showed two bars of signal. Then one. Then none.

At the Willits exit, he pulled over to check his supplies one more time. The Coleman sleeping bag was wedged behind the passenger seat next to a backpack that held everything he could afford: granola bars, a water filter he'd found at Goodwill, his father's old multi-tool, waterproof matches in a tin that still smelled faintly of tobacco, a compass, and a notebook. Not enough for any real journey, but then again, he wasn't planning a real journey. Just a day hike. Maybe two.

Sure you are, a voice in his head whispered. It sounded like his own, but older. Wiser. *That's why you withdrew your last hundred dollars in cash. That's why you didn't tell anyone where you're going.*

He pushed the thought away and merged back onto the highway.

The landscape transformed completely over the next hour. The hills grew steeper, the trees taller. Fog crept down from the mountains, turning the world soft and dreamlike at the edges. Every mile seemed to peel away another layer of the modern world. Billboard advertisements became sparse, then disappeared entirely. Cell towers vanished behind ridgelines. Even the highway itself seemed to narrow, as if reluctant to continue into this older, wilder country.

Near Leggett, he passed a sign: "ENTERING HUMBOLDT COUNTY." The fog thickened immediately, as if the boundary meant something more than lines on a map.

His GPS screen went completely black.

Micah pulled into the next turnout, hands trembling slightly as he dug out the printed directions he'd had the foresight to bring. Old school. His father would have been proud. The paper showed a simple route: Highway 101 to exit 663, then east on a forest service road for twelve miles. The trailhead would be marked.

Marked by what? he wondered. In his dreams, there had been a wooden sign, weathered and full of bullet holes. But dreams weren't reliable navigation aids.

Except these dreams had led him to real coordinates. Real missing persons reports. Real warnings from park services about restricted areas.

He started the car again, noting how the engine sounded different here—smaller, almost muffled by the weight of the surrounding forest. The fog pressed closer, limiting visibility to maybe fifty feet. Other cars appeared and vanished like ghosts. Twice, he could have sworn he saw figures standing by the side of the road, but when he looked directly, there was nothing but trees.

The exit appeared suddenly, barely visible through the fog. "663 - FOREST ACCESS." Micah turned east, leaving the highway's relative safety behind.

The forest service road was narrow, poorly maintained. His Honda's suspension protested every pothole and washout. The fog was so thick now he could barely see ten feet ahead. He dropped to fifteen miles an hour, then ten, navigating more by instinct than sight.

The trees crowding the road weren't like the oaks and eucalyptus back home. These were giants—Douglas firs and the first true redwoods, their trunks disappearing into fog above and darkness below. They seemed to lean over the road, creating a tunnel that grew narrower with each mile.

His odometer showed he'd been on the service road for eight miles. Then nine. The road deteriorated further, becoming barely more than a dirt track. At ten miles, he stopped to check the directions again, certain he must have missed a turn.

That's when he noticed the silence.

No bird songs. No wind in the trees. Even the Honda's engine, still running, seemed muted. The fog pressed against the windows like something solid, alive.

Micah turned off the engine and sat in the sudden, complete quiet.

The pull in his chest was stronger now, almost painful. Not forward anymore, but to the right, directly into the forest where no road led. He looked at the printed directions again. Two more miles to the official trailhead.

But every instinct told him he was already there.

He grabbed his backpack from the rear seat, checking its contents one more time. Sleeping bag strapped to the bottom. Water bottles full. Granola bars that would last maybe two days if he rationed them. The weight felt both insignificant and final.

Before he could talk himself out of it, Micah locked the car and stepped into the fog.

The cold hit him immediately, different from the normal northern chill. This was the cold of deep places, of caves and shadowed groves that never saw direct sunlight. He zipped his jacket higher and looked back at the Honda. Already it seemed insubstantial, more memory than metal.

The forest called to him from the right, where no trail should be.

But there was a trail. Faint, overgrown, but unmistakably there. As if it had been waiting.

Micah shouldered his pack and started walking, leaving the last pretense of the ordinary world behind. The fog closed in behind him, and within ten steps, he could no longer see his car.

The trees rose around him and somewhere in the distance—impossible to say how far in this muffling fog—he could hear the collective internet screaming at him:

Don't wander off the marked paths! Seriously.

The trail wound through fog so thick it felt like walking through clouds. Micah had been following it for twenty minutes, each step taking him deeper into a world that felt increasingly separate from the one he'd left behind. The path seemed to know where it was going even if he didn't, turning and climbing with purpose.

Then, without warning, the fog began to lift.

Not completely—wisps still clung to the higher branches—but enough that Micah could finally see where he was. The forest opened into a small clearing, maybe thirty feet across, carpeted with redwood sorrel and sword ferns. Shafts of sunlight, the first he'd seen in an hour, slanted down through breaks in the canopy.

And there it was.

The sign stood at the far edge of the clearing, exactly as he'd dreamed it. Weathered wood, probably once painted brown and yellow in the Park Service style, now faded to gray. The letters were barely legible, but Micah didn't need to read them. He'd seen them a hundred times in sleep:

DANGER - RESTRICTED AREA - PERMIT REQUIRED BEYOND THIS POINT

Bullet holes peppered the lower portion—three clustered near the left corner, one dead center. Someone had carved initials into the post: *RT + MM 1987*. A peace symbol. A crude drawing that might have been a tree or a person with raised arms.

Micah's hands shook as he pulled out his phone to take a picture. Still no signal, but the camera worked. He framed the shot, trying to capture the way the trail continued past the sign, disappearing between two redwoods so massive they could have been pillars holding up the sky.

A sound made him turn—footsteps on the trail behind him.

A young couple emerged from the fog, moving fast. Too fast for hikers enjoying a morning walk. The woman was blank-faced, a shell-shocked expression like someone who had stumbled into a horror movie when they thought they were going to see Disney.

"Hey," Micah called out. "Is everything okay?"

They didn't acknowledge him. Didn't even seem to see him. They hurried past, giving the sign a wide berth, heading back the way Micah had come. The woman stumbled once, and the man caught her elbow, whispered something urgent. Then he turned, his gaze falling hard on Micah's face.

"Whatever you're looking for in there, kid, it's not worth it."

The words were spoken kindly, the way a teacher might speak to a student holding a cigarette and a spray paint can.

"What if I'm not looking for anything?" Micah asked. "What if something's looking for me?"

The man stared at him for a long moment. Then he shrugged and continued down the trail after the woman. "Then God help you," he called back without turning. "Because nothing else will."

Then they were gone, swallowed by the fog.

Micah stood alone in the clearing, heart hammering. The rational part of his mind—the part that had kept him safe for twenty-one years—screamed at him to follow them. To get back in his car and drive home. To forget this whole insane idea.

But the pull in his chest had become almost painful now. And looking at the trail beyond the sign, he felt a certainty that went deeper than thought. This was why he'd come. This was what he'd been called to find.

Micah stood alone again. The forest beyond the sign seemed to breathe, a subtle movement of mist and shadow that made the trees appear to shift when he wasn't looking directly at them. The pull in his chest had become almost unbearable, like a fishhook tugging at his sternum.

He thought about the ranger station he'd seen online, the permits he was supposed to get, the twenty-four-hour wait, the video the rangers showed warning of missing people.

Then he thought about going back to his apartment. To the overdue bills and the dead phone and the endless, gray weight of a life that felt like drowning in slow motion.

A raven called from somewhere beyond the sign, a harsh sound that could have been laughter or warning.

Micah hitched his backpack higher and walked to the sign. Up close, he could read the faded text below the main warning:

Forest Service Order No. 05-07-51-19

Violation Punishable by Fine and/or Imprisonment

Under 16 U.S.C. 551, 36 CFR 261.53

He didn't have money to pay a fine. And would prison be worse than his life? Hard to say.

His hand trembled as he reached out to touch the weathered wood. It felt older than it looked, smooth in places where countless other hands had touched it. Contemplated it. Made their choice.

The moment his fingers made contact, the forest beyond seemed to shimmer. Just for a second, like heat waves off summer asphalt. The trees rearranged themselves in that instant—or maybe his perception of them did. The trail that had seemed narrow and overgrown suddenly looked clearer, more inviting. Welcoming, even.

Come home, a voice whispered. Not his father's this time. Older. Female. Familiar in a way that predated memory.

Micah pulled his hand back, heart racing. The forest returned to its previous configuration—dark, mysterious, clearly dangerous.

But the pull remained. Stronger than ever.

He looked back the way he'd come. The fog had thickened again, erasing the path completely. Forward, past the sign, the air seemed clearer. As if the restricted area existed in its own pocket of reality.

Which was insane. Completely insane.

But so was driving six hours north because of a dream. So was feeling more alive standing at the edge of danger than he'd felt in two years of safe, gray existence.

Micah took a deep breath that tasted of pine resin and something older, earthier. He pulled out his phone one more time, typing a message to David that would never send: *Following something I can't explain. If I don't come back, know that I chose this. That for once in my life, I chose something.*

Then he stepped past the sign.

The change was immediate but subtle. The temperature dropped five degrees. The quality of light shifted, becoming somehow older, as if filtered through amber. His phone screen flickered once and went black—not powered off, but dead in a way that suggested it would never work again.

Behind him, he heard the sound of wind through trees, though the air around him was perfectly still.

When he turned to look back, the sign was still there. But beyond it, where the clearing should have been, there was only more forest. Dense, impenetrable, ancient.

The trail he'd walked to get here was gone.

The massive redwoods rose on either side like living walls, their bark deeply grooved and russet in the strange amber light that filtered through the canopy.

He'd been walking for twenty minutes since passing the sign, and the world had transformed completely. The fog that had choked the access road didn't exist here. Instead, the air was crystalline clear but somehow thick, as if it carried more weight than normal atmosphere. Each breath tasted of resin and moss and centuries.

His father's compass—tucked in the side pocket of his backpack—had been his first indication that the rules were different here. He'd pulled it out after five minutes of walking, wanting to maintain some sense of direction. The needle had spun lazily, clockwise, then counter-clockwise, then faster until it was a blur of motion that made him dizzy to watch. He'd put it away, understanding on some instinctive level that navigation here would require different tools.

The silence was the second sign. Not empty silence—the forest was full of presence—but an absence of the sounds that should exist. No birds. No small animals rustling through undergrowth. No wind in the canopy high above. Only his footsteps, which seemed both too loud and somehow muffled, as if the forest was listening but absorbing the sound.

He paused at what might have been the half-hour mark—his watch had stopped the moment he'd crossed the threshold, its hands frozen at 2:23 PM. The trail split here, or seemed to. The main path continued straight, winding between more massive trees. But to the left, a fainter track led into a grove where the light fell differently, golden and inviting.

"Okay," he said aloud, just to hear a human voice. The word fell flat, swallowed by the acoustic dampening of the place. "Message received."

He kept walking.

At what felt like an hour in, though time had become negotiable, the trail began to climb. The trees grew even larger, if that was possible. Some of the redwoods were so massive that the trail wound between their exposed roots, creating natural archways that forced him to duck. The bark was soft to the touch, almost warm, and more than once he could have sworn he felt a pulse beneath his palm.

Then the path crested a small rise and opened into a sight that stopped him cold.

A grove of giants spread before him, trees that dwarfed even the massive redwoods he'd been walking among. These were the titans, the old growth that had never known an axe, that had been ancient when Rome fell. They stood in a rough circle, creating a natural cathedral whose ceiling was lost in mist two hundred feet above. Shafts of sunlight, impossible given the time of day and the thick canopy, slanted down at perfect angles, illuminating the space with the kind of light that belonged in dreams.

And in the center of the grove, someone was waiting.

Micah's heart lurched, but as he stepped closer, he realized it wasn't a person. It was a shirt. A red North Face jacket, hung carefully on a branch at head height. Below it, arranged with deliberate precision, sat a pair of hiking boots, and a water bottle.

Micah's hands shook as he photographed the scene with his dead phone—muscle memory making him try despite knowing it wouldn't work. The items weren't weathered. They looked like someone had them there in the last day. The jacket looked new, the boots barely worn.

But the strangest thing was the arrangement itself. This wasn't the chaos of someone lost or injured. This was deliberate. Ritualistic. Like an offering.

Or a warning.

A sound made him spin around—footsteps on the trail behind him. But the path was empty. The footsteps continued, growing closer, the rhythm unmistakably human. Micah backed against one of the giant trees, bark rough against his palm, and waited.

The footsteps stopped directly in front of him.

The air shimmered, like heat distortion, and for just a moment he saw—or thought he saw—a figure.

Then the shimmer was gone, and Micah was alone again with the abandoned clothes and the impossible light.

He forced himself to breathe slowly, to think. The rational part of his mind offered explanations: hallucination brought on by stress, by the strange atmosphere, by oxygen deprivation at altitude. But this didn't feel like altitude. If anything, the air felt too rich, too full of something that wasn't quite oxygen.

When he looked back at the arranged belongings, they had changed. The jacket was faded now, weathered. The boots showed years of exposure.

Who had left their clothes there? And when?

Micah backed away from the memorial—for that's what it was, he realized, a memorial to someone who hadn't died but hadn't survived either—and continued on the main trail. There was no question of turning back. Even if the path behind him still existed in any meaningful way, the pull forward had only grown stronger.

The forest changed as he walked. Not dramatically, but in accumulating details. The trees began to show their true age—not just old, but ancient in a way that hurt to contemplate. Some had bark patterns that looked almost like faces, features suggested in the whorls and ridges. Others had grown together, fused into structures that defied individual classification.

The undergrowth changed too. The familiar ferns and sorrel gave way to plants he didn't recognize, though they felt familiar in a bone-deep way. Flowers that seemed to track his movement. Moss that glowed faintly in the shadows.

Mushrooms in perfect fairy rings that his feet seemed to avoid without conscious thought.

The trail began to descend, winding through groves where the light fell in impossible colors—not just gold now, but subtle shades of green and blue that had no source he could identify. His shadow sometimes fell in directions that made no sense given the slanted sunlight. More than once, he glimpsed movement in his peripheral vision, but when he turned there was only the suggestion of motion, like the afterimage of something that had just stopped dancing.

Then, as suddenly as it had begun, the descent ended at a stream.

Crystal clear, running over stones that looked like polished jade, with a sound that was almost musical. The trail continued on the other side, but there was no bridge, no stepping stones. Just the water, perhaps knee-deep, flowing from somewhere deeper in the forest.

Micah knelt at the bank, suddenly aware of his thirst. He'd been walking for... hours? Days? The frozen watch was no help, and the light hadn't changed in any way that suggested the passage of normal time. But his body knew it needed water.

He hesitated. Every fairy tale he'd ever read warned against drinking from strange streams. But his water bottles were finite, and something about this water called to him in the same way the forest had.

He cupped his hands and drank.

The water was cold, almost painful, and it tasted of minerals and moonlight and something else, something that made his vision swim for a moment. When it cleared, the forest looked different. Not changed, but more itself. As if he'd been seeing it through dirty glass that had suddenly been wiped clean.

Colors were deeper. Edges were sharper. And in the spaces between the trees, he could see...

He blinked hard, and the visions faded. Almost.

Standing, Micah looked at the stream again. Crossing it would be another threshold, he understood. The sign had been the first. This was the second. How many more before he found what he was looking for?

Or before it found him?

He sat on a fallen log to remove his boots and socks, rolling his pants up to his knees. The water, when he stepped in, was exactly as cold as he'd expected but somehow also warm, a sensation that made no sense but felt true. The current was stronger than it looked, tugging at his ankles with intent.

Halfway across, he caught sight of the trail once more, beckoning him to finish the crossing. And then he was on the other side, feet on dry ground though he hadn't climbed the bank yet, boots somehow back on though he didn't remember pausing to step back into them.

One foot in the front of the other. He strode up the hill, away from the stream, confident now in his journey, excited to see where it led.

At the crest of the hill, the trail died without warning.

One moment Micah was following a clear path between the ancient trees, the next he was standing in unmarked forest floor, staring at an unbroken carpet of moss and ferns. He turned slowly, looking for any sign of the way he'd come, but the forest stretched identically in every direction. No stream, no meadow.

"No," he said aloud, the word swallowed instantly by the acoustic void. "No, no, no."

He backtracked—or tried to. But after fifty steps in what should have been the right direction, nothing looked familiar. The trees, which had seemed to follow a clear pattern just moments before, now stood in configurations that hurt to parse, as if geometry itself had become negotiable.

Panic rose in his throat, sharp and metallic. He'd been so focused on following the pull, on the mystical weight of crossing thresholds, that he'd forgotten the most basic rule of hiking: always know your way back.

Except there was no way back. He understood that now with a clarity that was almost worse than confusion. The forest had allowed him in, but it had closed the door behind him.

Micah forced himself to stop moving, to breathe. Panic would kill him faster than anything else out here. He mentally inventoried his supplies: two water bottles, mostly full. Six granola bars. A bag of trail mix. The water filter that might or might not work on whatever streams existed in this place. His father's matches.

If he rationed carefully, he had maybe three days of food. Less if he was hiking hard. The water would last a day, two at most.

He checked his phone out of habit. Still dead, the screen reflecting his face in black glass. The compass spun lazily

when he pulled it out, then faster, then came to a stop point-
ing straight down.

"Okay," he said, trying to sound calm. "Okay. Think."

But what was there to think about? He'd spent his whole
life cocooning himself in the safest option, of always choosing the easy path, of coloring inside the lines—and this was
where his first real choice had led him.

He'd never gotten properly drunk, not even in college
when everyone else was discovering their limits. Never tried
drugs beyond the single hit of a joint that had made him par-
anoid at a freshman party. Never skipped class except when
his parents died, and even then he'd emailed his professors
with proper documentation. Never stayed out past midnight
unless you counted the nights he'd worked late shifts at the
diner, and that was just trading one responsibility for another.

His idea of adventure had been trying Ethiopian food once
with Sarah, and he'd ordered the mildest thing on the menu.

And now here he was, lost in a forest that didn't follow
the rules of reality, all because he'd been so desperate to feel
something—anything—that he'd literally walked into a place
people disappeared from.

The laughter bubbled up from somewhere deep, bitter
and helpless. "Great job, Micah," he told the trees. "Really
showed them all, didn't you? Showed them you could make
a choice. Showed them you weren't afraid. And look where
it got you."

The trees absorbed his words without echo, patient and
indifferent.

He started walking again because standing still felt like drowning. No direction seemed better or worse than any other, so he chose what might have been east, if directions meant anything here. The forest continued unchanging—beautiful, terrifying, utterly alien. More than once, he could have sworn he was walking in circles, passing the same distinctive trunk or fallen log, but when he looked closer the details were always different.

Time passed—an hour, maybe two. His water bottle emptied. The granola bar he'd eaten without thinking sat heavy in his stomach. The pack straps dug into his shoulders, and his feet began to ache in boots that had seemed comfortable enough in the store.

That's when he realized he hadn't just lost the trail. He'd lost the sound of water too. That musical stream he'd drank from—gone. The forest was teaching him a lesson about trust, about what happened when you followed voices into the dark.

The light never changed. That was the worst part. No way to tell if it was noon or evening, if he'd been walking for hours or minutes. The amber glow remained constant, sourceless, maddening. His shadow fell in different directions depending on which trees he passed, as if each giant had its own personal sun.

Thirst began to build. Why hadn't he filled his water bottles in the stream? Even though he'd drunk so greedily from it, he now felt like he had ashes in his mouth. He rationed his second water bottle, tiny sips that did nothing but remind him how dry his throat was becoming. The forest air seemed to pull moisture from him, leaving him desiccated despite the obvious dampness of the place.

A memory surfaced: his father teaching him to find water in the woods behind their old house. "Listen for it," he'd said. "Water always makes noise. And look for game trails—animals know where the water is."

But there were no game trails here. No sign that anything lived in this tomb of trees besides the trees themselves.

And him.

He hadn't seen a single living creature since entering the forest. No birds. No squirrels. No insects. Not even spiders in the ferns. Just the plants and the silence and the growing certainty that he was going to die here, another memorial of abandoned gear for some future dreamer to find.

Would they arrange his belongings carefully, like the memorial he'd seen? Would his wallet lie open to his driver's license, proof that Micah Thorne, age 21, had made one brave, stupid choice in his careful life?

He stopped walking, legs suddenly too heavy to continue. The moss looked soft here, inviting. He could rest for just a moment. Close his eyes. Maybe when he opened them, he'd be back in his apartment, this all a vivid dream brought on by depression and gas station coffee.

That's when he saw the fox.

It stood at the edge of his vision, perhaps thirty feet away, watching him with eyes that caught the amber light and threw it back like molten gold. Red fur seemed to glow against the green backdrop of ferns, and for a moment Micah thought he was hallucinating.

Then it tilted its head—a gesture so perfectly vulpine and yet somehow human in its curiosity—and he knew it was real. As real as anything could be in this place.

"Hey," he said softly, not wanting to spook it.

The fox continued to watch him, unafraid but keeping its distance. There was an intelligence in its gaze that made Micah's skin prickle. This wasn't just a fox that had wandered into the wrong forest. This was something that belonged here, that knew the rules and the paths and the secrets.

Slowly, never breaking eye contact, the fox turned and began walking deeper into the forest. After a few steps, it paused, looked back over its shoulder at Micah. The message was clear: *Follow, or don't. Your choice.*

Micah hesitated. Following mysterious animals in fairy tales never ended well. Well, sometimes it did. In *The Lion, the Witch, and the Wardrobe*, some of the animals were good. But not all of them. Of course, dying of thirst in a haunted forest definitely wouldn't end well. And something about the fox felt... not safe, exactly, but purposeful. Like it had been waiting for him to reach this point of desperation.

He shouldered his pack and took a step toward where the fox had been. It immediately moved further away, maintaining the distance between them. Another few steps from Micah, another measured retreat from the fox.

A guide that wouldn't let him get too close. Fair enough.

They moved through the forest this way for what felt like an hour—the fox appearing and disappearing between the massive trunks, always visible just long enough to show direction before vanishing again. It never let him close the gap, maintaining that careful thirty-foot buffer, but it never left him behind either.

The trees grew even larger, if that was possible, but spaced farther apart. The underbrush thinned. And then, so faint he thought he was imagining it, Micah heard the sound of water.

His pace quickened involuntarily. The fox seemed to approve, moving faster now, its red form flickering between the trees like flame. The sound grew louder—not the musical stream from before, but the simple, beautiful noise of water running over stones.

They emerged into a small clearing where a creek no wider than Micah's arm span flowed between moss-covered banks. It wasn't the same stream he'd seen before, but the water was just as clear—clear enough to see every pebble on the bottom, and the sight of it made his throat constrict with need.

The fox sat on the opposite bank, watching as Micah dropped to his knees and drank. The water was cold, mineral-rich, perfect. He drank until his stomach hurt, then filled both water bottles, then drank again.

Only when his thirst was satisfied did he look up to thank his guide.

The fox was gone.

Micah sat back on his heels, looking around the clearing. The light was finally beginning to change, taking on a deeper quality that might have been evening. Or might have been the forest deciding it was time for night, regardless of what the actual sun was doing beyond the canopy.

He needed to make camp. Build a fire while he still had light to gather wood. The matches in his pack felt suddenly precious—his last real link to the civilized world, the promise of warmth and light in the coming darkness.

As he began gathering fallen branches, Micah found himself searching the shadows for a glimpse of red fur. The fox was out there, he was certain.

He thought about the couple fleeing in tears, about the abandoned clothes, about all the warnings he'd ignored. But he also thought about the pit in his stomach whenever he imaged going back to his apartment.

Maybe following a mysterious fox through a haunted forest wasn't the worst choice he'd ever made.

Chapter 4: The First Night

The fallen redwood branch was thick as Micah's thigh, dry despite the forest's perpetual dampness. It would burn hot and long. His father's voice echoed in his memory, teaching him to choose fuel. *Pick the dead wood that snaps clean, not the soft stuff that crumbles. Look for resin beads that catch fire like promises.*

He'd forgotten he knew these things. Forgotten that his body remembered what his mind had let slip away. The motions came back unbidden—arranging tinder, building the kindling teepee, saving the thick branches for later. His father's matches sat in their tin, three dozen wooden stems that smelled of sulfur and old tobacco.

The clearing by the creek was small but defensible, if that word meant anything in a place where the rules kept shifting. A massive redwood had fallen here ages ago, its trunk creating a natural windbreak on one side. The creek curved around the other, its constant murmur a comfort after the oppressive silence of his lost wandering.

Micah worked methodically, gathering wood while the strange amber light still held. The undergrowth yielded plenty of dry kindling—twigs and small branches that had somehow avoided the moisture that should have rotted them long ago. Each piece he selected felt significant, as if the forest was allowing him these small gifts.

The fox was nowhere to be seen, but Micah felt its presence, its gaze. Watching. Evaluating. He'd grown up with the suburban foxes that raided garbage cans and denned under porches, clever but ultimately mundane creatures. This fox was something else entirely. The intelligence in its golden eyes had been almost human, but not quite. Something older. More patient.

He arranged his wood with care his father would have approved of—kindling in the center, graduating to finger-thick branches, then the larger pieces radiating outward like spokes. The ritual of it calmed him, gave his hands something to do besides shake.

The matches were in a tin that had survived twenty years in his father's camping gear, then two more in storage. The metal was worn smooth by handling, the hinges stiff with disuse. Inside, the matches lay in neat rows, each one promising light and warmth despite decades of neglect. Micah counted them—thirty-six. If he was careful, if he kept the fire going through the night and relit it each evening, he might have enough for a month.

A month. The thought should have terrified him. A month in this place that didn't follow the rules of reality. A month of rationing granola bars and filtering water that might not be entirely water. A month of following a fox that might be leading him deeper into whatever had swallowed all those missing hikers.

He felt only a strange calm at the thought of it, far removed from the oily panic he felt at the idea of returning to his apartment, or even to his car.

The first match caught immediately, the sulfur flare sharp in his nostrils. He touched it to the nest of dried moss and bark shavings he'd prepared, watched the small flame catch and spread. Fed it carefully with twigs no thicker than pencil lead, then gradually larger pieces as the fire found its strength.

By the time full darkness fell—if darkness was the right word for the way the amber light simply deepened into bronze, then copper, then something that had no name—his fire was crackling steadily. The warmth pushed back the chill that had been creeping into his bones since he'd crossed that final stream.

Micah sat cross-legged on the moss, back against the fallen redwood, and watched the flames dance. The smoke rose straight up, disappearing into the canopy that was now just a suggestion of darker darkness above. No wind disturbed it. No breeze carried it away. The smoke simply ascended until the forest swallowed it, like everything else.

He should eat something. His stomach had been growling for the last hour of gathering wood, a mundane complaint that seemed almost funny in this decidedly un-mundane place. But he had six granola bars. And no idea how long he'd be here, or if the forest would provide anything edible.

One bar tonight, he decided. Tomorrow he'd need to figure out foraging. The fox had led him to water—maybe it would show him food as well. Or maybe that wasn't its purpose. Maybe it was simply ensuring he survived long enough for... whatever came next.

He pulled out a granola bar, chocolate chip, the wrapper crinkling impossibly loud in the silence. The forest seemed to lean in at the sound, as if curious about this artifact from another world. Micah tore it into thirds, ate one piece slowly, savoring the sweetness that tasted too intense, too real. Everything here was like that—turned up past normal, saturated with meaning he couldn't quite grasp.

"So," he said aloud, needing to hear a human voice even if it was only his own. The word fell into the darkness beyond the firelight and vanished without echo. "Here we are."

The silence that answered wasn't empty. It was full of attention, maybe even anticipation. The hair on the back of his neck rose, but he forced himself to stay still, to breathe normally. Panic was a luxury he couldn't afford.

That's when he saw the eyes.

They appeared at the edge of the firelight, twin points of reflected flame floating at the height of his seated head. The fox. It had returned, or perhaps it had never left. It sat just beyond the circle of warmth, watching him with that unsettling intelligence.

"Thank you," Micah said softly. "For the water. I would have..." He trailed off. Would have what? Died? Maybe. Or maybe the forest would have provided another way. Or maybe dying was the point, and the fox had interrupted some larger plan.

The fox tilted its head, a gesture so perfectly animal yet with an all-to-human intelligence behind it. In the firelight, its red fur seemed to glow with its own inner flame, edges blurring into the darkness as if it wasn't entirely solid. Or entirely here.

"Are you going to sit there all night?" Micah asked. "You could come closer. I don't bite."

The fox's mouth opened slightly, an almost-smile. Then it lay down, sphinx-like, still maintaining that careful distance. Close enough to watch. Far enough to vanish if needed.

Micah ate the second third of his granola bar, then wrapped the remainder carefully and tucked it back in his pack. The fire popped, sending sparks spiraling upward. He fed it another branch, watched the flames accept the offering and grow.

The warmth was making him drowsy despite the strangeness of everything. Or maybe because of it. There was something hypnotic about the flames, about the way they moved in patterns that seemed almost like language. His eyelids grew heavy.

He forced them open. Sleeping seemed dangerous, even with the fire, even with the fox standing guard. But his body had other ideas. The exhaustion of the day—had it only been one day since he'd left his apartment?—crashed over him like a wave.

Micah pulled out his father's sleeping bag, unrolling it close to the fire. The fox watched every movement with interest. The bag smelled of storage and old smoke and something indefinable that was purely his father—coffee and WD-40 and the particular soap he'd used.

"If I fall asleep," Micah told the fox, "and something comes to eat me, at least make it quick."

The fox's eyes sparked with something that might have been amusement.

Micah crawled into the sleeping bag fully clothed, only removing his boots. The ground was softer than it should have been, the moss beneath him yielding like a mattress. Another gift from the forest, or another trap? At this point, what was the difference?

He lay on his side, facing the fire, where he could see the fox in his peripheral vision. The creature hadn't moved.

The fire crackled and whispered. The creek murmured its endless story. And somewhere in the darkness beyond the light, things moved with careful steps, curious about the newcomer but not yet ready to introduce themselves.

Micah's eyes drifted closed despite his best efforts. The last thing he saw was the fox, outlined in flame, standing guard at the edge of the light. The last thing he heard was his father's voice, carried on no wind:

You always were stubborn. Took you long enough to get here.

The fire had burned down to embers when Micah found himself in that strange territory between sleep and waking. The fox still sat at the edge of the dying firelight. He should add more wood. The thought drifted through his mind without urgency. But his body felt heavy, weighted down by exhaustion and something else—the peculiar sense that he needed to be still and wait.

In the darkness beyond the clearing, something whispered his name. The sound of wind through needles, of water over stone, of time moving in directions he'd never learned. The fox's ears twitched toward the sound, but it didn't otherwise react. Whatever called to him was known here. Expected, perhaps.

Micah forced his eyes fully open, pushed himself up on one elbow. The sleeping bag rustled, too loud in the quiet. He reached for a piece of wood, added it to the embers. The fire accepted it grudgingly, smoke curling up before small flames began to lick at the bark.

"Can't sleep either?" he asked the fox, voice rough with almost-sleep.

The fox tilted its head, that gesture he was beginning to recognize as acknowledgment. In the renewed firelight, Micah could see it more clearly. Its coat was perfect, un-marred by the burrs and debris that should have clung to any animal moving through dense undergrowth. The red fur seemed to hold its own light, subtle but undeniable.

Another whisper from the darkness. Closer this time. The fox's attention never wavered from Micah.

He sat up fully, sleeping bag pooling around his waist. The air had grown colder, or perhaps that was just his imagina-tion. Everything here felt negotiable, including temperature. He pulled his jacket tighter, grateful he'd kept it on.

The granola bar wrapper in his pocket crinkled as he moved. Such a mundane sound, yet it seemed to offend the forest's ears. The whispering stopped immediately, as if caught in the act of something improper.

"I know you're there," Micah said to the darkness. "Whatever you are."

Silence answered him.

Minutes passed. Or hours. The fire burned steadily now, pushing back the dark in a small circle of warmth and light. Beyond that circle, the forest waited.

Then, at the very edge of perception, movement—a shift.

The air shimmered, heat distortion without heat, and for just a moment Micah saw, or thought he saw, a figure standing between the trees. Tall, translucent, wearing clothes that belonged to no era he recognized. Then the shimmer passed and there was only forest again.

His heart hammered against his ribs. The fox turned its head to look where the figure had been, then back to Micah. Its expression (could a fox have an expression?) seemed to say: *Yes, you saw what you saw. No, I won't explain it.*

"Is this what happened to them?" Micah asked, not really expecting an answer. "The missing hikers? Did they see things too?"

The fox blinked slowly, a gesture that felt like acknowledgment and dismissal combined.

Micah fed the fire another branch, watching the flames grow. The warmth was real, at least. That had to count for something. His water bottles sat beside his pack, still full from the creek. His stomach rumbled, reminding him of the last piece of the granola bar still wrapped in his pocket. But he didn't eat it. Not yet. The night felt too strange for something as ordinary as eating.

Instead, he pulled out his notebook and pen. He'd brought them thinking he might want to record his thoughts, maybe write some kind of farewell letter that would never be sent. Maybe something for the park rangers to find when they inevitably came looking. Now, holding the pen, he found himself sketching the fox.

He wasn't much of an artist, but something about the firelight and the strange clarity of exhaustion guided his hand. The fox emerged on the page in rough lines—the alert ears, the intelligent eyes, the way it sat with such perfect stillness. As he drew, he noticed details he'd missed before. The white tip on its tail. The darker fur around its muzzle. The way its front paws crossed, almost delicate.

When he looked up from the drawing, the fox was closer.

Not by much—maybe five feet. But definitely closer. Micah hadn't heard it move, hadn't seen it shift position. One moment it had been at the edge of the firelight, the next it was within the circle of warmth.

"Curious?" Micah asked, holding up the notebook.

The fox's eyes tracked to the page, studied it with what looked like genuine interest. Then those amber eyes met his, and Micah felt the full weight of that ancient intelligence. This wasn't just a fox. It was something else wearing fox shape, or perhaps a fox that had become something more by virtue of living in this impossible place.

He set the notebook aside, moving slowly, telegraphing every motion. The fox watched but didn't retreat.

"I don't suppose you could tell me what happens next," Micah said. "Where we go from here. What I'm supposed to do."

The fox's mouth opened in that not-quite-smile again. Then it looked pointedly at the fire, at the sleeping bag, at Micah himself. The message was clear: *Rest. Morning will come. Things will be clearer then.*

Or at least, that's what Micah chose to read into the gesture. He could have been projecting human meaning onto animal behavior. But nothing about this fox felt merely animal.

He added one more log to the fire, a thick piece that would burn slow and long. Then he lay back down, pulling the sleeping bag up to his chin. The fox settled into its sphinx position again, now close enough that Micah could see the rise and fall of its breathing.

"Thank you," he said again. "For staying."

The fox's ear twitched.

Micah closed his eyes, listening to the crack of the fire, the murmur of the creek, the deep silence of the forest. Sleep crept up on him again, softer this time, less like drowning and more like sinking into warm water.

Just before he went under completely, he could have sworn he heard his father's voice again, carried in the rustle of branches: *The forest teaches everyone. The question is whether you'll survive the lessons.*

But maybe that was just the beginning of dreams. In a place like this, who could tell the difference?

The fox kept watch as Micah slept, its amber eyes reflecting the firelight, seeing things in the darkness that human eyes weren't meant to perceive. Once, it turned its head sharply toward the north, ears pricked at some sound beyond human hearing. But whatever it sensed chose not to approach, and the fox resumed its patient vigil.

The dream took him gently. Micah found himself standing by the same fire, in the same clearing, but everything was subtly wrong. The flames burned without consuming wood. The creek flowed upward, defying gravity with liquid grace. And across from him, where the fox should have been, sat his father.

Not translucent like before. Not ghostly or ethereal. Solid as the earth, wearing the flannel shirt Micah had forgotten existed until this moment. The fabric was worn soft at the elbows, missing the third button down—details too specific for ordinary dreams.

"You always were stubborn," his father said, and his smile was sad and proud in equal measure. "Took you long enough to get here."

"Get where? Dad, what is this place?"

His father gestured at the darkness beyond the fire, a motion that encompassed everything and explained nothing. "Where the debt comes due. Where the pattern can be broken. Where we finally stop running."

The words felt heavy, weighted with meaning Micah couldn't quite grasp. He tried to stand, to reach across the fire, but his dream body wouldn't cooperate. He was rooted in place, able only to watch and listen.

Behind his father, another figure materialized from smoke and memory. Grandfather James, wearing his dress uniform but lacking the thousand-yard stare that had defined him in life. His face was younger than Micah had ever seen it, unlined by war and its aftermath.

"Every generation thinks if they can run fast enough, they'll escape it," his grandfather said, voice rougher than his son's, carved by cigarettes and screams. "Your great-grandfather thought moving west would be the answer. I thought Korea would burn it out of me. Your father thought..."

"I thought love would be enough," his father finished. "That if I loved your mother hard enough, loved you deep enough, it would build a wall between you and what we carry."

"What do we carry?" Micah's voice came out younger than it should have been, unwinding his development into a man.

His two forbearers exchanged a look that spanned generations of shared understanding. Then his father leaned forward, the firelight casting strange shadows across his face.

"Sin compounds interest," he said. "Old sins. The kind that echo through blood and bone. We've all been running, son. Running west like every American family with something to hide. Running to war, running into bottles or work or early graves. But the forest—" He gestured again at the darkness. "The forest is where you stop running."

"Or where you get lost forever," his grandfather added, not unkindly.

Behind them, Micah could see other shapes forming from smoke—great-grandfather Harold in his factory clothes, great-great-grandfather William in a minister's collar that seemed to choke him. A line of Thorne men stretching back into darkness, each carrying something broken, something that wouldn't heal.

The fire flared suddenly, impossibly bright. When Micah's vision cleared, his father and grandfather were fading, becoming translucent as the dream began to fracture.

"Wait," Micah called. "I don't understand. What am I supposed to do?"

His father's voice came from very far away, already more echo than sound: "Trust the guide. It knows the way through. We never had one."

"Dad!"

But they were gone. The fire was normal fire again, burning low, consuming wood like fires should. The creek flowed in its proper direction. And across from him, the fox sat watching with those amber eyes that held too much intelligence for a simple animal.

Micah gasped awake, heart racing. The real fire had burned down to coals that glowed like dragon eyes in the darkness. He fumbled for wood, added two pieces with shaking hands. As the flames caught and grew, he looked for the fox.

It was closer now, maybe ten feet away, sitting in that same sphinx position. Watching. Waiting. When their eyes met, the fox nodded—a small motion, but unmistakably deliberate.

"You're the guide," Micah said, voice hoarse. "That's what he meant. You're going to show me... what? The way out? "

The fox tilted its head, neither confirming nor denying.

Micah pulled his knees to his chest, wrapping his arms around them. The sleeping bag had twisted during his restless dreams, leaving him half-exposed to the cold. But he didn't adjust it. The chill helped ground him in what was real—or as real as anything could be in this place.

"Sin compounds interest," he repeated his father's words. "Old sins." He thought of the family pattern his mother had mapped out—all those early deaths, all those men who never made it past forty. His great-grandfather Harold, fleeing Massachusetts for California after some scandal. The newspaper clipping about embezzled church funds. Earlier ancestors with their own religious disasters—excommunications, fraud, always something rotten where faith should have been.

The fox's ears pricked forward, attentive.

"My family and religion ," Micah said, half to himself. "Like oil and water."

Well, part of his family anyway. His cousin David's family had been the opposite. The "churchy" faction of the family. Something remarked upon with both disdain and jealousy by his dad... and by Micah himself.

The fox stood suddenly, a fluid motion that brought it another few feet closer. Now Micah could see details that the darkness had hidden—the white fur inside its ears, the delicate black lines around its eyes like kohl. It was beautiful in the way wild things were beautiful. Perfect and dangerous and utterly itself.

The hours that followed passed in a strange rhythm of vigilance and exhaustion. Micah fed the fire methodically, rationing his wood supply while keeping the flames high enough to push back the darkness. The fox remained alert, occasionally turning its head toward sounds Micah couldn't hear, its ears tracking movements in the forest that never materialized into visible threats.

He pulled out his notebook again, needing something to occupy his hands and mind. The sketch of the fox stared back at him from the page, crude but recognizable. Below it, he began to write, documenting the strangeness of this place before it could fade like a dream.

The trees here are older than old. Not just ancient—prehistoric. Like they remember when the world was different. When maybe the rules were different.

Water that tastes like moonlight. Paths that exist until you need to go back. Time that moves like honey or lightning depending on its mood.

And the fox. Red fur that glows with its own light. Eyes that know things. It saved me today—led me to water when I was lost. Now it guards me from... something.

His pen paused.

The fox made a soft sound—not quite a bark, more like a conversational murmur. When Micah looked up, it was watching him write with apparent interest.

"Can you read?" he asked, feeling only slightly ridiculous. In a place where streams flowed upward in dreams and voices spoke from empty darkness, a literate fox seemed almost reasonable.

The fox tilted its head, then deliberately looked at the notebook, at Micah, at the fire. Its meaning seemed obvious: *Less writing. More watching. The night isn't over.*

Micah closed the notebook but kept it on his lap, the pen still in his hand. The weight of it was comforting—proof that the regular world still existed, even if he'd stepped outside its boundaries.

"My father said you know the way through," he said to the fox. "Through what? To what?"

The fox's amber eyes reflected the firelight, turning them into small suns. It didn't answer—couldn't answer—but something in its steady gaze suggested patience. *All things in time. First, survive the night.*

A branch cracked somewhere in the darkness, loud as a gunshot in the silence. The fox was on its feet instantly, every muscle tense. Micah's hand tightened on his pen, absurdly thinking he might defend himself with it.

But no circling footsteps followed. No voices from the void. After a long moment, the fox settled again, though its alertness never fully relaxed.

"Was that normal forest sounds?" Micah asked. "Or something else?"

The fox's ear twitched. If it could have shrugged, Micah thought it would have.

He shifted position, trying to ease the ache in his back from sitting on the ground. The moss was softer than it should have been, but it was still the ground. His body, used to a mattress and the controlled environment of his apartment, protested the conditions. But there was something else too—a vitality he hadn't felt in years. As if the forest air, thick with whatever made this place impossible, was waking parts of him that had been sleeping.

Or dying.

The thought came unbidden, unwelcome. Had he been dying back there? Not physically—he was young, relatively healthy despite the diet of convenience store food and irregular sleep. But something in him had been shutting down, system by system. The part that hoped. The part that planned. The part that believed tomorrow could be different from today.

Here, in this impossible forest with its guardian fox and stalking shadows, he felt more alive than he had since—

Since his parents died.

The realization hit him like cold water. For two years, he'd been going through the motions of living without actually being alive. And it had taken walking into a place that might kill him to remember what living felt like.

The fox made another sound, drawing his attention. It had moved again while he was lost in thought, now sitting close enough that he could have reached out and touched it without fully extending his arm. Its eyes held something that might have been understanding.

"You know about loss," Micah said quietly. "Don't you? You know about carrying weight that gets heavier every day."

The fox blinked slowly, a gesture that felt like acknowledgment.

"Is that why you're helping me? Because you recognize—" He gestured vaguely at himself, at the forest, at the whole impossible situation. "Whatever this is?"

The fox turned to look at the fire, then back at Micah. Then, in a movement so deliberate it couldn't be mistaken for anything but communication, it looked at the eastern sky where the canopy was thickest, then at the ground, then at Micah again.

Dawn will come. Rest. I'll watch.

Or maybe he was just projecting meaning onto animal behavior. But the message felt clear enough. Micah had been awake for hours now, feeding his anxiety along with the fire. His body needed rest, even if his mind raced.

"You'll wake me if something comes?" he asked.

The fox's stare was answer enough.

Micah reluctantly lay back down, pulling the sleeping bag up to his chin. The fire crackled steadily, well-fed enough to last a few hours. The fox sat between him and the darkness, a guardian in red fur.

Despite everything—or perhaps because of it—sleep came easier than expected. His last conscious thought was how strange it was to trust his life to a wild animal he'd met mere hours ago. But then again, he'd trusted his life to far less reliable things. Jobs that didn't value him. An apartment that was slowly killing him. The promise that if he just kept going through the motions, someday it would get better.

At least the fox was honest in its strangeness. At least this forest, for all its dangers, didn't pretend to be anything other than what it was.

He dreamed again, but gentler dreams this time. His mother sitting at the kitchen table, surrounded by genealogy documents, trying to piece together a puzzle with missing pieces.

But the dream shifted before she could say anything, dissolving into images of trees growing in fast-forward, centuries passing in heartbeats. Of men walking westward, always westward, carrying burdens that bent their backs but never quite broke them. Of churches rising and falling, their doors always slamming shut if he approached.

When Micah woke, the first pale suggestion of dawn was filtering through the canopy. Not true sunlight—he doubted direct sun ever reached the forest floor here—but a gradual lightening that turned black to gray to green.

The fire had burned down to coals, but the fox was exactly where it had been when he fell asleep. It turned to look at him as he stirred, and something in its expression suggested satisfaction. They'd made it through the first night. Whatever came next, that was an accomplishment.

"Thank you," Micah said, voice rough with sleep. "For keeping watch."

The fox stood, stretched in a way that was purely animal, then looked meaningfully at the creek. *Water. Drink. The day begins.*

Micah couldn't argue with that logic. He climbed out of the sleeping bag, joints protesting, and made his way to the creek. The water was shockingly cold against his face, clearing away the last cobwebs of sleep. He drank deeply, refilled his bottles, then returned to the camp.

The fox was standing at the edge of the clearing, looking into the forest with obvious expectation. When Micah approached, it took a few steps forward, then looked back.

Time to go. Deeper. Forward. The first night was just the beginning.

Micah looked at his small camp—the remnants of the fire, the flattened moss where he'd slept, the evidence of his first night in this impossible place. It had been a kind of home, however temporary. Leaving it felt like another threshold.

But that's what he'd come here for, wasn't it? To cross thresholds. To go deeper. To find whatever waited for him.

He shouldered his pack, checked that his father's matches were secure, that his water bottles were full. The remaining granola bars felt pitifully inadequate for whatever lay ahead, but the fox had found him water. Perhaps it would find him food as well.

"Lead on," he said to the fox.

It gave him one last long look—assessment? warning? encouragement?—then turned and walked into the forest. Not quickly, always staying within sight, but with clear purpose.

Micah took one last look at the clearing that had sheltered him through his first night in the Shadow Grove. Then he followed his guide into the deepening green, into whatever the second day would bring.

The fox led him away from the creek, following no path that Micah could discern. They wove between massive trunks, the fox's red form flickering in and out of sight but never quite disappearing. The forest floor was soft with centuries of fallen needles, muffling their footsteps until they moved in near silence.

As they walked, Micah noticed the forest changing around them. The bark patterns grew more complex, whorls and ridges that suggested meaning just beyond comprehension.

The spaces between trees took on deliberate arrangements, as if planned by an ancient landscaper.

The fox paused at a hollow formed by the roots of a particularly massive redwood. Inside, barely visible in the dim morning light, mushrooms grew in a perfect spiral. They glowed faintly, a phosphorescence that belonged more to deep ocean creatures than forest fungi. The fox looked at them, then at Micah, then continued on without explanation.

The fog came up from the earth like breath.

Micah had grown accustomed to strange weather in the days since entering the forest, but this was different. The mist rose in slow spirals from the ground itself, threading between ferns and pooling in the hollows of roots, thickening until the world beyond ten feet became suggestion rather than fact. The fox paused on the path ahead, its red coat muted to rust by the gray light, and waited for him to catch up.

His legs ached with the particular weariness of sustained effort on insufficient fuel, but he doubled his effort, striving to keep going.

The fox began moving again, picking its way along a path that was less path than absence of obstacle. Micah followed. He had learned not to question the route, not to wonder why they curved around certain trees or paused at particular stones. The fox knew things he did not. That was the nature of guides.

Then he heard it.

At first, he thought it was the wind finding some hollow in the canopy, some natural flute of bark and air. But the sound refined itself as he listened, separating from the general murmur of the forest into something distinct. Something that made his heart stutter in his chest.

A voice. Calling his name.

Micah.

It was neither shout nor whisper, just his name, spoken the way someone might speak it across a kitchen table. The way his mother used to speak it when dinner was ready, when she wanted to show him something in the garden, when she had no particular reason at all except that she liked to say it.

He stopped walking. The fog had thickened while he wasn't paying attention, and now it pressed against him like damp cloth, cool on his face and hands. The voice came from somewhere to his left, off the path, deeper into the gray where the trees became ghosts of themselves.

Micah, honey.

His mother's voice. He would have known it anywhere, would know it if he lived a thousand years. The particular music of it, the way she stretched the first syllable of his name. She had been gone for two years, buried next to his father in a cemetery he barely visited, and yet here she was, calling him through the fog like she had something important to tell him.

He took a step toward the sound before he knew he was moving.

The fox materialized in front of him so quickly it might have been there all along. It stood directly in his path, head low, body tense, and when Micah tried to step around it, a sound came from its throat, a rumble that vibrated in his chest like a struck chord. A warning.

"That's my mother," Micah said. His voice came out strange, rough from disuse. He hadn't spoken aloud in days. "I hear her."

The fox did not move. Its amber eyes held his with an intensity that was almost painful, and Micah understood that this was not accident, not the random behavior of an animal. The fox was telling him something.

Stay on the path.

But the voice came again, and this time there was something underneath it. A note of worry, perhaps. The particular tone his mother used when he was running a fever, when he had scraped his knee, when she was trying to find him in a crowded store.

Where are you, sweetheart? I can't see you.

The fog swirled between the trees, and for a moment Micah thought he saw movement in it. A shape, like someone waiting just beyond the edge of visibility. His chest ached with wanting to go to her, to wrap his arms around her one more time, to tell her all the things he had never said while she was alive.

The fox growled again, and this time its lip pulled back just slightly, showing teeth that gleamed like wet bone. Not threatening him, exactly. But making clear that this was a threshold, and crossing it would mean something.

Micah stood in the space between the path and the fog, and he felt the choice pressing down on him. He had come to this forest because something in his blood demanded it, because generations of Thorne men had heard its call and answered or fled or died. He had trusted the fox to lead him this far, through days of hunger and strangeness and fear.

But this was his mother's voice.

He looked at the fox. He looked at the fog. He thought about all the stories where people followed beautiful sounds into darkness and were never seen again. He thought about how grief could make you believe anything, how badly he wanted something, anything, to be true.

The voice came once more, fainter now, drifting away as if the fog itself was carrying it.

Micah...

And then it was gone. The fog remained, thick and silent, but the calling had stopped. The forest held its breath, waiting to see what he would do.

Micah closed his eyes. He let himself feel the loss of it, the specific cruelty of hearing her voice and being unable to follow. He let the grief move through him like water through cloth, soaking everything, leaving nothing dry. His mother was dead. She was not in this fog. Whatever had been calling to him wore her voice like a borrowed coat, and he would not follow it into the gray.

He opened his eyes and looked at the fox.

"Okay," he said. "Okay."

The tension went out of the animal's body like a released spring. It turned and continued up the path without waiting to see if he followed, but Micah thought he saw something in the way it carried its tail. Approval, perhaps.

The fog began to thin as they walked, and slowly the forest reassembled itself around him. Trees became solid again, their bark textured and real. The path widened. Somewhere above, a bird called out in a voice that was only a bird's voice, nothing more.

Micah's heart still ached with the ghost of his mother's words. It would ache for a long time, maybe forever. But he was still walking. He was still on the path. And somewhere ahead, the fox was leading him toward whatever waited at the center of all this strangeness.

He did not look back. Though in the hours that passed in silence after that, Micah turned the encounter over in his mind, until finally, the memory was forced from his mind at the sight of what waited for him over the next gentle rise.

At the crest, Micah stopped, breath catching in his throat.

A grove spread below them, but calling it a grove seemed inadequate. It was a natural amphitheater, trees arranged in concentric circles around a central space where morning mist pooled like milk in a bowl. The scale was impossible—each tree a titan, their combined presence creating something that felt more like architecture than nature.

The fox sat at the edge of the overlook, giving Micah time to absorb what he was seeing. In the center of the grove, barely visible through the mist, something stood. A stone? A structure? The fog obscured it, revealing only suggestions of straight lines that didn't belong in a forest.

"Is that where we're going?" Micah asked.

The fox turned to look at him, then back at the grove. Not today, its posture suggested. But eventually. When you're ready.

They skirted the edge of the grove, keeping to the higher ground. As they walked, exhaustion began to creep into

Micah's bones and he felt his heart sink in dreadful anticipation when the fox led him to a small clearing where a massive oak had fallen, its trunk split lengthwise by some ancient lightning strike. The two halves lay parallel, a natural resting place. Micah sat heavily on one of the logs, dropping his pack with relief.

The moment his eyes closed, the vision took him.

He stood in the same clearing, but it was different. Older. Newer. The light had a sepia quality, like old photographs. His grandfather stood before him, but not the grandfather from the previous night's dream. This was Grandfather James in his prime, wearing work clothes instead of his uniform, shoulders broad and hands calloused.

"You see it?" his grandfather asked, gesturing at the split tree. "The burden?"

Micah looked more carefully. The fallen oak wasn't just split—it had been prepared. Rope lashed the two halves together at one end, creating a crude travois. The kind of thing you could drag behind you, if you were strong enough. If you were willing.

"Every man has to carry his own," his grandfather said. His voice carried the weight of hard-won knowledge. "Can't leave it for the next generation. Can't pretend it ain't there. You pick it up, you drag it as far as you can. That's the only way through."

Micah could see scratches in the dirt where others had dragged similar burdens, grooves worn deep by repetition. A well-worn path of suffering voluntarily undertaken.

"But what if I can't?" Micah heard himself ask. "What if it's too heavy?"

His grandfather's expression hardened. "Then you die here. And your son after you. And his son. The burden don't disappear just because you won't lift it. It just gets heavier."

The vision shifted. Micah was alone now with the split tree and its rope harness. He approached it tentatively, wrapped the rough rope around his shoulders. Tried to lift.

The weight was impossible, the pain of it threatening to tear parts of him loose. He could feel the accumulated mass of generations of failure, of sin unconfessed, of easy choices that led to hard consequences.

He pulled harder, managed to drag it a few inches. The effort sent fire through his muscles, made his vision blur. This wasn't just wood and rope. This was every time he'd taken the easy path. Every job interview missed. Every opportunity avoided. Every moment he'd chosen comfort over growth.

Sarah's voice echoed from memory: "*You never try, Micah. Never. It's like you're afraid of what happens if you actually put in effort.*"

The rope burned his palms. Another few inches. His father's voice now: "*It's okay to fail, son. But you have to try first.*"

But it was too hard. Too heavy. Micah let the rope slip from his hands, stumbled backward. The split tree thudded back to earth, and he felt the impact in his chest like judgment.

"I can't," he whispered to the empty clearing. "I'm sorry, I just can't."

The vision began to fade, but not before he saw them—shadowy figures stretching back through the trees. His father, his grandfather, his great-grandfather, all the men of his line who had stood in this same place, faced this same choice. Some had bloodied their hands on the rope before giving up. Others hadn't even tried.

None had carried it all the way through.

Micah gasped back to consciousness, still sitting on the actual split log. The fox sat a few feet away, watching him with those ancient eyes. Waiting.

His hands ached though he hadn't moved them. When he looked down, faint red marks crossed his palms where dream-rope had burned.

"Was that real?" he asked the fox. "Any of it?"

The fox tilted its head toward the split tree he sat on. Real enough, the gesture said.

Micah stood on shaking legs, looked at the fallen oak with new eyes. Someone had prepared it, just like in the vision. The rope was gone—rotted away or taken—but the marks remained. Grooves where bindings had been. Scratches in the earth that might have been drag marks, softened by time but not erased.

"Is that why you brought me here?" he asked, but he wasn't sure if he was talking to the fox or the forest itself. "To show me I'm just like them? Too weak, too afraid to do the hard thing?"

The fox made no response, just watched with infinite patience.

Micah thought of all the times he'd chosen the easy path. Dropping out of college instead of pushing through grief. Taking the diner job instead of pursuing something meaningful. Letting Sarah go without fighting for the relationship. A lifetime of small surrenders that had led him here, to a forest that seemed determined to show him exactly who he was.

"Maybe that's what this place does," he said, voice bitter. "Shows you the truth about yourself. Makes you see what everyone else already knows—that you're a coward. A failure. A waste."

The spiral of self-loathing was familiar, almost comfortable. How many nights had he lain in his apartment, cataloging his failures? But here, in this impossible forest, the weight felt heavier. More real.

"Is that why they disappear?" He was talking to himself now, pacing the clearing. "The hikers who never come back? They see themselves clearly for the first time and realize the world is better off without them?"

He thought of the arranged clothes, the careful memorials. Not victims of the forest but volunteers. People who'd walked into the green cathedral and decided not to walk out.

"Maybe that's why I'm here," he said, the words tasting like copper in his mouth. "Not to break some curse or find some redemption. Just to finally do one thing right. To stop pretending I'm going to suddenly become someone different, someone better."

The fox stood abruptly, a sharp movement that cut through his spiral. It walked to the edge of the clearing, looked back at him, then sat. Waiting. Always waiting.

"What's the point?" Micah asked it. "I couldn't lift it. Couldn't carry the burden. Just like my father couldn't. Just like none of us could. What's the point of going deeper when we already know how it ends?"

The fox's amber eyes held no judgment, no disappointment. Just that eternal patience. It would wait for him to decide. The forest would wait. They had nothing but time.

Micah sat back down on the split log, head in his hands. But even as despair settled over him like fog, some small part of him noticed: the fox hadn't left. It could have abandoned him here, decided he wasn't worth guiding. But it waited.

Maybe that meant something. Maybe not. But it was what he had.

After a long time, Micah stood. His legs felt weak, his spirit weaker. But standing was something. Moving was something.

The fox stood, stretched, and began walking. Not back the way they'd come, but forward. Deeper. The choice, as always, was Micah's—follow or stay. Face whatever came next or remain in this clearing with its split tree and its impossible weight.

He thought of his apartment, of the gray existence he'd fled. Of his father in the morgue. Of all the Thorne men who'd died young.

Maybe he'd fail too. Maybe the forest had brought him here to show him that failure, to let him choose his ending with full knowledge of what he was.

But the fox was walking, and he'd come this far.

Micah shouldered his pack—so light compared to that split tree—and followed.

The clearing fell behind them. He was weak. He was afraid. He was everything his family's pattern had predicted.

But he was still walking.

Chapter 5:
The Grove of Eyes

The second day brought a different kind of silence. Micah had grown accustomed to the forest's quiet—that dense, absorptive hush that swallowed sound like water swallowing stones. But this was something else. This silence had texture to it, as if the air itself had thickened into something that pressed against his eardrums, filling the space where birdsong and wind should have been with a presence that was somehow louder than noise.

The fox walked ahead of him, picking its way between roots that rose from the ground like the fingers of buried giants. Its ears rotated constantly now, swiveling toward sounds Micah couldn't hear, tracking movements in the undergrowth that produced no visible source. Three times in the last hour, it had stopped without warning, body tense, head turned toward some point in the darkness between the trees. Each time, Micah had frozen behind it, heart hammering, waiting for whatever had caught the fox's attention to reveal itself.

Nothing had. Nothing visible, anyway. But the fox's wariness had infected him, and now he walked with his shoulders hunched and his breath shallow, every nerve singing with the particular alertness of prey that knows it's being watched.

The path wound through a section of forest that looked no stranger than anything else he'd seen thus far, but felt different. The trees, bent and blended together, their ancient wood beckoning him, drawing his gaze deeper with each turn—when he heard it for the first time.

Not a voice. Not exactly. It came from somewhere to his left, from the deeper shadows between two massive redwoods whose canopies had grown together A breath. A word that dissolved before he could catch its meaning.

Micah stopped walking. The fox had stopped too, he realized—had stopped before him, its body gone rigid, its fur standing slightly along the ridge of its spine. It was looking in the same direction he was. Toward the shadows. Toward the almost-sound.

"Did you hear that?" he whispered, and immediately felt foolish. Of course the fox had heard it. The fox heard everything.

The whisper came again. Closer now, or seeming to be. It wound through the undergrowth like smoke, threading between ferns and pooling in the hollows of roots. He couldn't make out words—wasn't sure there were words—but there was rhythm to it. Cadence. The rise and fall of speech stripped of its consonants, leaving only the ghost of meaning.

More voices joined the first. Or perhaps it was the same voice, multiplied, reflected off bark and stone until it surrounded him. They came from everywhere and no-where, overlapping, interweaving, creating a texture of almost-language that made his skin crawl with the effort of trying to understand.

The fox's ears pinned back against its skull. It took a step backward, pressing its shoulder against Micah's leg. The warmth of its body was a small comfort against the cold that had begun seeping into his bones. Not physical cold, though the temperature had dropped. This was the cold of being watched by something that didn't have eyes. Of being spoken to by something that didn't have a mouth.

"What is it?" Micah asked, and his voice came out thin, cracked, the voice of a boy who had wandered too far from home and realized, too late, that home was a concept that no longer applied.

The fox didn't answer. Couldn't answer. But it pressed harder against his leg, and he understood: *Stay still. Don't follow the voices. Don't try to find where they're coming from.*

Easier said than done. The whispers had a pull to them, a gravity that tugged at something deep in his chest. They weren't calling his name—he was almost certain of that—but they were calling *something*. Some part of him that wanted to answer. Some hollow place that recognized itself in the sound of voices that existed at the edge of existence.

The whispers grew louder. Or maybe he was listening harder. They seemed to come from inside his own skull now, from the space behind his eyes where thoughts formed before becoming words. They spoke of rest. Of release. Of laying down the burden he'd been carrying since before his parents died, since before Sarah left, since before he'd understood that some weights couldn't be set down because they had become part of the person carrying them.

His foot moved toward the shadows without his permission.

The fox bit him.

Not hard—just a sharp nip at his ankle, teeth through sock and skin, enough to shock him back into his body. He gasped, looked down, found those amber eyes staring up at him with an intensity that brooked no argument. The fox's lips were pulled back slightly, not quite a snarl but a warning. *Stay here. Stay present. Whatever they're offering, it isn't yours to take.*

The whispers seemed to sense his hesitation. They shifted, changed pitch, became something almost plaintive. Almost familiar. For one terrible moment, he thought he heard his mother's voice in the chorus—her particular way of saying his name, the music of it that he had almost forgotten in the two years since her death.

"Mom?" The word escaped before he could stop it.

The fox pressed harder against his leg. Its whole body was trembling now, whether from fear or effort he couldn't tell. It was fighting something, he realized—not physically, but in some other way. Holding a line. Keeping the whispers from crossing whatever threshold separated their world from his.

And it was working. Slowly, painfully, the voices began to recede. Not because they chose to, but because the fox's presence was somehow anathema to them. Its warmth against his leg, its teeth still resting lightly against his ankle, its amber eyes fixed on the shadows with an ancient defiance—these things created a barrier the whispers couldn't cross.

The almost-sounds faded. The texture of the silence changed, becoming merely empty rather than pregnant with meaning. The shadows between the trees remained shadows, nothing more. The cold ebbed from Micah's bones, replaced by the ordinary chill of forest air that hadn't seen direct sunlight in centuries.

He realized he was crying. When had that started? His face was wet, his breath hitching in his chest, his whole body shaking with the aftermath of something he couldn't name. The whispers hadn't hurt him, but they had touched something. Had reached into the hollow places inside him and found exactly what they were looking for.

The fox released his ankle and stepped away, but only a few feet. It sat facing him, watching his breakdown with that patient intelligence that had guided him through everything so far. No judgment in its gaze. No impatience. Just witness.

"Thank you," Micah managed, his voice rough with tears. "I almost—I don't know what I almost did. Followed them. Went into the dark. Let them have whatever they wanted."

The fox tilted its head. *Yes. You almost did. But you didn't.*

"What were they? The voices?"

But the fox only turned and began walking again, following the non-path through the ancient trees. The conversation, such as it was, had ended.

Micah wiped his face with the back of his hand and followed.

He walked more carefully now, more deliberately. The whispers had shown him something about himself—about the part of him that wanted to stop trying, stop carrying, stop being. That part was larger than he'd realized. It had been growing in the dark of his depression, feeding on the grief and failure and loneliness until it had become something almost separate from himself. Something that recognized the voices as kin.

The fox led on. Micah followed. The whispers did not return, but he could feel them out there in the spaces between trees, patient as stone, waiting for the moment when his resolve weakened enough to let them in.

He would not give them that moment. Not today.

Tomorrow was a different question. But tomorrow hadn't come yet.

The path wound deeper into the ancient woods, and after a time—impossible to say how long. The air took on a different quality, heavy with attention, as if the forest itself had turned its gaze toward him.

And then, rounding a massive trunk that must have been growing when Rome still ruled the Mediterranean, he saw them.

Eyes. Dozens of them. Set into bark like knots that had split open to reveal something watching. Or were they watching? In the amber light, Micah couldn't be sure if the patterns were ancient carvings worn smooth by centuries or something alive that moved when he looked away.

In the center of the circle, the fox sat beside stones arranged in a pattern that hurt to comprehend—spirals within spirals, each rock placed with impossible precision.

Behind him, the entrance to the grove had already sealed itself with undergrowth that looked decades old. Vines thick as his wrist wove between saplings that hadn't existed moments before. The forest had closed its door. Forward was the only direction left.

The fox remained perfectly still, waiting. Not urging, not demanding. Simply present, as if it had all the time in the world. Because it did, Micah realized. Whatever schedule he thought he was on, whatever human urgency had driven him here, meant nothing in this place.

He took a step forward. The eyes tracked his movement, hundreds of them blinking in slow waves that rippled around the circle. Another step. The ground beneath his feet felt different here—not quite solid, as if the earth itself was deciding whether to support his weight.

The stones at the grove's center pulled at him. Not physically, but with the same inexorable draw that had brought him to the forest in the first place. Symbols carved deep into their surfaces seemed to writhe in his peripheral vision, settling into stillness whenever he looked directly at them. They predated language, predated writing, but somehow he understood their purpose. They were a question. A test. A judgment.

His stomach cramped, empty and angry. When had he eaten last? The hunger made everything sharper and more distant at the same time. Made it hard to trust what he was seeing. But the fox was real—he'd followed it here. The eyes might be carvings animated by exhaustion and starvation, but the fox was real.

Wasn't it?

Another step. The air grew thicker, like walking through invisible curtains. Each forward movement required more effort, more commitment. The trees leaned inward, their watching eyes now close enough that he could see details— whorls of bark that formed pupils, cracks that suggested irises, patterns that were too deliberate to be accidental.

"I'm here," he said aloud, voice cracking from disuse. "Whatever you want from me, I'm here."

The words fell flat in the strange acoustics of the grove, swallowed before they could echo. But something shifted. The resistance in the air eased slightly. The eyes blinked again, considering.

The fox stood, stretched with casual grace, and walked to the very center where the carved stones waited. It sat again, tail wrapped around its paws, and fixed Micah with a look that managed to be both patient and expectant.

There was no path through the watching trees except the one that led to those stones. No choice but forward or a slow death trapped at the edge of something he didn't understand. Micah thought of all the careful years behind him, all the safe choices that had led him to this supremely unsafe place. His father had played it safe too. Worked his job, paid his bills, followed the rules. Died at thirty-nine anyway.

Maybe safety was the trap. Maybe the only way out was through.

He walked toward the center, each step watched by those impossible eyes. The symbols on the stones grew clearer as he approached, though they still defied understanding in any language he knew. They seemed to shift between meaning and meaninglessness, hovering just beyond comprehension like a word on the tip of his tongue.

The fox moved aside as he reached the stones, giving him room to approach while maintaining its watchful presence. Up close, the rocks were older than they'd appeared from the edge—worn smooth in places by countless years, but with carvings that looked fresh as yesterday. The central stone, larger than the others, bore a spiral that seemed to descend forever into its surface.

Micah knelt before it, legs grateful for the respite. The eyes in the trees had gone still, no longer blinking, waiting for something. The forest itself seemed to hold its breath.

He reached toward the stone, hand trembling from more than hunger. The moment before contact stretched before him, time doing that strange thing it did here where seconds could feel like hours. Then his palm touched the warm surface, and everything changed.

Understanding flooded through him—not in words but in bone-deep knowing. The stone was asking something. Testing something. The symbols weren't language but pure meaning, stripped of the need for translation:

What do you carry that isn't yours?

The question reverberated through him, shaking loose things he'd buried so deep he'd forgotten they were there. The grove waited. The eyes watched. The fox sat motionless as carved stone itself.

And Micah understood that lying wasn't possible here. Whatever this place was, whatever power animated it, it would know. The truth would come out of him whether he wanted it to or not. The only choice was whether to offer it willingly or have it torn from him.

He opened his mouth to speak, and the forest leaned in to listen.

The stone hummed with a frequency he felt in his teeth. Words appeared in his mind, not heard but known: *What do you carry that isn't yours?*

Micah opened his mouth to speak and found he couldn't lie. The truth pulled itself out of him like a splinter working free. "My father's depression. My grandfather's war. My great-grandfather's shame. All of them dead too young, and me—I'm carrying their ending like it's already written. Like I'm already dead and just don't know it yet."

The words hung in the amber air, more real than anything he'd said in years. His voice sounded strange to his own ears, raw and honest in a way that would have embarrassed him in the world beyond the trees. But here, pretense had no power. The grove demanded truth, and truth was all he had left to give.

"I carry their failures," he continued, unable to stop now that he'd started. "Every man in my family who couldn't make it past forty. Every dream they gave up on. Every bottle they turned to. Every time they chose the easy wrong over the hard right. I've been carrying it since before I was born."

The stone's warmth increased under his palm, not burning but intense enough to make him want to pull back. He didn't. Couldn't. The connection held him in place while the grove sorted through his words, weighing them on scales he couldn't see.

"I carry Sarah's disappointment. That last look she gave me, like I'd failed some test I didn't know I was taking. I carry every job application I was too scared to send. Every opportunity I let rot because trying felt like setting myself up for the failure I knew was coming. I carry—"

His voice broke. Tears he hadn't shed at his parents' funeral, hadn't shed when Sarah left, hadn't shed in all the gray months since, suddenly burned their way free. They ran down his face, and he tasted salt and truth and years of deferred grief.

"I carry their ghosts," he whispered. "All of them. The dead and the living who might as well be dead to me. I carry them like stones in a bag, adding one more with every year that passes. And I'm so tired. So fucking tired of weight that was never mine to begin with."

The humming from the stone changed pitch, became something almost like music. The fox, which had been still as a statue, turned its head to look at him. In its amber eyes, Micah saw something that might have been approval. Or understanding. Or simple acknowledgment that yes, this was the truth it had been waiting to hear.

The symbols on the stone pulsed with soft light, then dimmed. The pressure that had been building in the grove— the sense of being evaluated, judged, measured—began to ease. Not disappearing entirely, but shifting from active interrogation to something more like recognition.

The eyes in the trees blinked again, but differently now. Less synchronization, more individual. As if whatever collective intelligence animated them was satisfied with his answer. Some of the eyes closed entirely, bark sealing over them until they were just knots and whorls again. Natural, ordinary.

Well, as ordinary as anything could be in a place where trees had eyes and stones asked questions.

Micah's hand slipped from the stone, and he sat back on his heels, exhausted by the confession. His whole body shook—from hunger, from emotional release, from the strange energy of the grove itself. He felt hollowed out, scraped clean, like a pot that had been scoured down to raw clay.

The fox stood and walked to the far edge of the grove. As it moved, Micah noticed what he hadn't before—an opening in the circle of trees. Not a path exactly, but a space where passage was possible. It hadn't been there when he'd entered. He was sure of it. The grove had been sealed, impenetrable.

But he'd answered the question. Passed the test. Told the truth about what he carried.

The fox paused at the opening, looking back at him with those patient amber eyes.

Micah pushed himself to his feet, legs protesting after kneeling on the hard ground. His pack felt heavier than before, though he'd eaten most of his food. Maybe some burdens became heavier the moment you acknowledged them.

He took one last look around the grove. Most of the eyes had closed now, leaving only a few watching his departure. The stones sat innocent and ordinary, just rocks arranged in a pattern that no longer hurt to perceive. Even the air felt different—still thick with that otherworldly quality that marked this place as separate from normal reality, but no longer actively hostile.

Micah shouldered his pack and followed the fox through the opening.

Beyond the grove, the forest transformed again. The trees here were older, if age could be measured in places where time moved like honey. Their trunks rose beyond sight, disappearing into a canopy so high it might have been the sky itself. Micah followed the fox through this cathedral of wood, each footstep careful on ground that felt more sacred with every yard.

He paused to lean against a tree, bark rough and real against his palm. The fox stopped immediately, looking back with those patient amber eyes. Always watching. Always waiting. Never pushing him faster than he could go, but never letting him stop entirely either.

"Just need a moment," Micah said, voice hoarse.

The fox sat, apparently content to wait. Its red fur caught what little light filtered through the canopy, making it glow like an ember against the green-black shadows of the forest floor. Watching it, Micah felt the hollow ache in his stomach sharpen into active pain.

His pack held one last granola bar. He'd been saving it, rationing it against some future hunger that would be worse than this one. But his hands shook as he reached for his water bottle, and he knew that future had arrived. He pulled out the bar, wrapper crinkling loud as gunshots in the cathedral quiet.

The fox watched him unwrap it, head tilted with what might have been curiosity. Did spirit guides understand human hunger? Did they know what it meant to need food, water, rest?

Micah ate slowly, trying to make it last. The processed oats and honey tasted like the finest meal he'd ever had. His body responded to the small gift of calories with pathetic gratitude, momentarily quieting the constant growl of his empty stomach. But he knew it wouldn't last. A hundred and forty calories against days of hiking, nights of cold, the constant energy drain of simply existing in this impossible place.

When he finished, he folded the wrapper carefully and tucked it into his pack. Leave no trace—his father's teaching, even here where the normal rules didn't apply. The fox stood as he pushed away from the tree, ready to continue their strange journey.

They walked for what might have been hours. Without the sun's movement or his phone's clock, Micah could only guess at the passage of time by the accumulating ache in his feet and the slow descent of light through the canopy. The forest here felt different from the sections he'd passed through before. Not hostile like the grove with its watching eyes, not desperately wild like the areas where he'd first gotten lost. This was forest that had never known human touch, that existed according to its own ancient logic.

Mushrooms grew in perfect spirals around certain trees. The fox led him past most of them, but at one particular spiral—the mushrooms golden as autumn leaves—it stopped and looked at him expectantly.

Micah knelt beside the fairy ring, studying the fungi. He knew nothing about mushroom identification. In the real world, eating random forest mushrooms was a quick way to poison yourself. But the fox had led him to water when he thirsted. Had led him through the watching grove. Had been his only constant companion in this place that defied constants.

He picked one of the golden caps, turned it over to examine the gills. It smelled of earth and autumn and something else, something that made his mouth water despite the risk. The fox watched, patient as always, offering no encouragement but no warning either.

Trust. That's what this was about. Trust in a guide that couldn't speak, couldn't explain, could only lead.

Micah bit into the mushroom. It tasted like the forest floor after rain, rich and complex and surprisingly filling. Not poisonous, or at least not immediately so. He ate two more, then stood to continue walking. The fox approved, or seemed to, turning to lead him onward through the ancient trees.

As they walked, memories began surfacing uninvited. Not the traumatic recollections the grove had pulled from him, but smaller things. Quieter things. His mother reading him bedtime stories, her voice soft in the darkness of his childhood room. His father teaching him to tie fishing knots, patient hands guiding clumsy fingers. Moments of connection before everything went wrong.

He wondered if the mushrooms were affecting him, if they contained some compound that loosened the boundaries between past and present. Or if the forest itself was drawing these memories out, examining him in its slow, thorough way.

The light continued its lazy fade toward what might charitably be called evening. The eternal twilight deepened by degrees, shadows pooling in the spaces between trees.

The pool appeared without warning. One moment Micah was following the fox through dense undergrowth, the next he stood at the edge of water so still it might have been polished obsidian. The surface reflected not the perpetual twilight of the forest canopy, but a sky he hadn't seen in days—clear, deep blue, with clouds that moved in directions the wind didn't blow.

The fox circled the pool's edge, agitated in a way Micah hadn't seen before. It wouldn't approach the water, wouldn't look directly at its surface. Instead, it paced the perimeter, occasionally glancing at Micah with what seemed like warning in its amber eyes.

But the pull was already there. Not like the grove's demanding presence. This was subtler. An invitation written in the perfect stillness of the water, in the way it reflected a sky that couldn't exist beneath such dense trees. The pool wanted to show him something.

Micah knelt at the edge, careful not to disturb the mirror surface. His reflection stared back—gaunt, bearded, eyes hollow with exhaustion and something else. Transformation, maybe. Or recognition of how much he'd already changed in just a few days.

Then the reflection shifted.

His father's face replaced his own, but younger. Twenty-two, maybe twenty-three. The same age Micah was now. The resemblance was uncanny—not just the features they shared, but the expression. That particular combination of fear and determination that came from carrying weight you didn't know how to put down.

"I can feel it in me," his father's reflection said, lips moving beneath the still water. "Like rust spreading through pipes. My father had it, his father before him. When does it stop? How do I keep it from my son?"

The water rippled, though Micah hadn't touched it. His father's image dissolved, replaced by another scene. Still his father, but older now, sitting in their garage with the car engine off. Micah recognized this—not from memory, but from his mother's journal. The day she'd found him there, staring at nothing, carrying on both sides of a conversation with someone who wasn't there.

"It's coming for me," his father said to the empty passenger seat. "Just like it came for all of them. And I'm going to pass it to him. My boy. My son. How do I break something that's in the blood?"

Another ripple. The scene shifted.

His grandfather appeared in the water, a young man in his twenties in combat fatigues that looked too big for his thin frame. He sat alone in what might have been a bunker, writing by candlelight. The letter in his hands shook as he wrote:

I did things today that can't be undone. I can feel them settling into my bones like shrapnel that will never work its way out. Maybe that's what we are—men who carry what we've done until it breaks us. Men who were broken before we were born.

The water showed him bodies in Korean mud. His grandfather's hands, impossibly young, covered in blood that wouldn't wash off no matter how hard he scrubbed. The moment when something essential broke inside him, creating a fracture that would define the rest of his short life.

Micah wanted to look away but couldn't. The pool held his gaze as surely as the grove's stone had held his hand.

Another shift. His great-grandfather Harold, standing in an empty church treasury, hands full of money that wasn't his. The calculation on his face wasn't greed but desperation. Behind him, through a window, Micah could see a woman holding a baby—his grandfather, infant and innocent, unaware that his father was about to paint a target on their bloodline that would last generations.

"God help me," Harold whispered, stuffing bills into a leather satchel. "But You won't, will You? You never do. Not for us."

The water rippled again, showing Harold on a train heading west, his family asleep around him. He stared out the window at a darkness that had nothing to do with night, everything to do with the weight of what he'd done. What he'd stolen. What he'd broken that could never be repaired.

Scene after scene flowed through the pool. Great-great-grandfather William, standing before a congregation that wouldn't meet his eyes. Great-great-great-grandfather Josiah, fleeing another town, another scandal, another failure of faith. Back and back, each generation carrying the wounds of the one before, adding their own failures to the pile.

But then Micah saw something else. In each scene, each moment of breaking, there was love too. Harold stealing to feed his family. His grandfather writing letters home that spoke of hope even from hell. His father trying so hard to be different, to break the pattern, even as it broke him.

The water stilled. His own reflection returned, but different now. He could see them all in his face—Harold's desperate eyes, his grandfather's clenched jaw, his father's worried brow. Generation after generation of accumulated trying and failing and trying again.

Micah pulled back from the water, gasping as if he'd been holding his breath. The fox stood at his shoulder—when had it moved so close?—warm and solid against his leg. An anchor to the present moment.

Taking the lead, the fox led him away from the pool along a path that seemed to materialize only as they walked it. Micah's legs moved of their own accord, his body operating on some reserve he hadn't known existed. The visions from the water still played behind his eyes when he blinked. He felt scraped hollow by what he'd seen, but cleaner for it. As if something rotten had finally been lanced.

The trees here grew closer together, their trunks fusing at the base like old friends leaning on each other for support. The spaces between them narrowed until he had to turn sideways to pass, the rough bark scraping against his pack, his shoulders. The fox slipped through easily, its smaller form unhindered, but it paused often to let him catch up.

Then the forest closed.

One moment there was space enough to move, and the next the trees stood shoulder to shoulder in every direction, a wall of bark and shadow with no gaps wide enough for a man to pass. Micah turned in a slow circle, searching for the path they'd been following, but it had vanished as if it had never existed. The fox sat a few feet away, watching him with those patient amber eyes, offering no guidance.

"Where do we go?" His voice came out thin, cracked. The fox only blinked.

Micah pressed his palm against the nearest trunk, feeling for some hidden passage, some trick of perspective. The bark was solid, real, unyielding. He moved to the next tree, then the next, his movements growing frantic. Every direction was the same. Trees packed so tightly their branches interlocked overhead, blocking even the twilight that had been his constant companion. The darkness here was absolute, broken only by the faint glow of the fox's fur.

His breath came faster. The old familiar panic rose in his chest, the same drowning sensation that had pinned him to his apartment floor on the worst nights. His heart hammered against his ribs. The trees seemed to lean closer, pressing in, reducing the small clearing to something like a cell. Like a grave.

"No." The word escaped him without thought. "No, no, no."

He dropped to his knees, hands pressed to the soft earth, trying to remember how to breathe. Had he failed a test? Was the forest boxing him in, never to let him out?

The panic crested and held, a wave that refused to break. Micah knelt in the darkness, surrounded by impossible trees, and felt every failure of his life pressing down on him. Every time he'd frozen instead of acted. Every door he'd let close because walking through it seemed too hard. He was going to die here, trapped in a circle of ancient wood, because he didn't know how to move forward.

The thought sat with him for a long moment. He let it.

Then something shifted within him.

A small, quiet voice that sounded almost like his mother's: *You've come this far. You passed the grove. You saw the truth in the water. Are you really going to stop now because there's no path?*

Micah lifted his head. The fox watched him, amber eyes reflecting light that had no source.

There had never been a path. Not really. The forest had made one appear when he needed it, had guided his feet when he trusted enough to follow. But trust wasn't passive. It wasn't just following a fox through the trees and hoping for the best. Trust was choosing to believe that the way forward existed even when you couldn't see it.

He stood slowly, legs unsteady but holding. The panic receded, and he looked at the wall of trees surrounding him, at the impossible barrier.

"I don't know where to go," he said aloud. The words felt strange in his mouth, an admission he'd spent his whole life avoiding. Asking for directions was weakness. Admitting confusion was failure. Real men figured things out on their own.

But he wasn't on his own. He had never been on his own here, not really.

Micah looked up, past the interlocked branches, toward whatever watched from above. "I need help," he said. "I want to keep going, but I can't find the way. Please. Show me where to go."

The silence that followed was vast and deep, the kind of silence that listens.

Then, from somewhere in the canopy, a sound. Not a rustle of leaves or crack of branch, but something alive. Micah held very still as the darkness above him shifted, rearranged itself, and the owl emerged from shadow like a thought taking form.

It was enormous. Larger than any owl had a right to be, its wingspan nearly brushing the trees on either side as it settled onto a low branch directly in front of him. Its feathers were the gray-brown of ancient bark, its eyes the deep gold of fossilized amber. It regarded him with an intelligence that felt older than the forest, older than language, older than the concept of paths and those who walked them.

The fox had gone still beside him, a deferential patience in its posture.

Micah met the owl's gaze. "Please," he said again.

The owl blinked once, slowly, like the closing and opening of a door. Then it spoke.

The sound that emerged was not a hoot, not exactly. It was a single word, low and resonant, shaped by a throat not meant for human speech yet producing something unmistakably linguistic. The syllables rolled through the darkness like stones dropped into still water:

"*Gwerthū.*"

The word meant nothing to Micah. It belonged to no language he had ever heard, no tongue still spoken by living mouths. But it carried meaning nonetheless, meaning that bypassed his ears and settled directly into his bones. He understood none of it and all of it at once.

The owl spread its wings.

The motion seemed to push the trees apart. The trunks that had stood shoulder to shoulder now leaned away from each other, creating a passage where none had existed. A path opened through the impossible wall, leading deeper into darkness that was somehow less absolute than the darkness behind him.

The owl held its wings extended for a moment longer, before taking off with a mighty flap of its wings, dissolving back into the shadows of the canopy as if it had never been more than a dream of feathers and gold eyes.

But the path remained.

The fox rose and stepped through the opening without looking back. Micah followed, and the moment he crossed the threshold, the air changed. Colder, thinner, carrying a quality he could only describe as proximity. As if something vast and incomprehensible had moved closer, was paying attention in a way it hadn't before.

He did not look back to see if the path closed behind him. He already knew it had.

The word stayed with him as he walked, burning in his chest like a coal that would not cool. *Gwerthū.* A threshold marked in syllables instead of stone. A gift given in exchange for the hardest thing he'd ever done.

He had asked for help. And help had come.

The light was fading faster now, what little filtered through the canopy taking on the deep gold of approaching night. The fox led him to a small clearing where fallen logs formed a natural shelter. Micah's body moved mechanically through the routine of making camp—gathering wood, arranging stones for a fire ring, his hands performing tasks they'd learned over these strange days while his mind still reeled from the pool's revelations. Each movement felt both automatic and profound, as if even these simple acts of survival had been transformed by what he'd seen. By the time he coaxed flame from one of his precious remaining matches, full darkness had claimed the forest.

They sat together by the dying fire—lost young man and spirit guide, watched over by trees older than memory.

His body was failing. His food was gone. His matches were dwindling. By any rational measure, he was dying slowly in a place that swallowed people whole.

But his spirit felt clearer than it had in years.

Tonight, exhausted and transformed, Micah slept beside the fire with his spirit guide warm against his side. He dreamed not of his ancestors' but of

men who'd learned to put down their burdens before those burdens buried them. He dreamed he stood among them, shoulder to shoulder, arm in arm. Strong beneath the weight they carried rather than crumbling. It was the strangest vision of the lot, simply because of how much he desired it, and how far away it felt.

Chapter 6:
The Unraveling

Micah woke to a world transformed.

The change struck him before he even opened his eyes—the air had teeth now, sharp and cold against his exposed skin. His breath emerged in white plumes that shouldn't exist, not in late October, not in California, not anywhere that followed the rules he'd spent his life learning.

He sat up slowly, joints protesting like rusted hinges, and stared at impossibility.

Snow dusted the ferns around his dead fire. Not much, just a fine layer like confectioner's sugar, but enough to rewrite everything he thought he understood. The moss that had cushioned his sleep now crunched beneath his palm, brittle with frost. Above him, the redwood canopy—that eternal green ceiling that had sheltered him for days—stood bare.

Bare. The word lodged in his throat like a stone.

Coast redwoods didn't lose their needles. They were evergreen, had been evergreen for millions of years before humans existed to name them. Yet here they stood, naked giants against a pewter sky, their branches sketched in charcoal strokes against clouds he'd never seen before.

"This isn't—" His voice cracked, unused and paper-thin. How long since he'd spoken? Days blurred together in this place where time moved like honey, sometimes racing, sometimes barely crawling. His last granola bar had been... yesterday? Two days ago? The hunger had shifted from demanding to simply present, a hollow ache that had become as familiar as breathing.

The fox sat ten feet away, a splash of autumn flame against the monochrome world. Its fur seemed brighter now, the only color that made sense, watching him with those amber eyes that held patience older than forests.

Micah's hands shook as he pushed himself to standing. The cold seeped through his jacket like water through cheesecloth but his shaking came from somewhere deeper, from the part of him that still insisted on rational explanations for irrational experiences.

"Redwoods are evergreen," he told the fox, as if saying it aloud would restore the world to its proper order. "They don't... they can't..."

But they had. Or he had. Or something had shifted in the night, sliding him sideways into a forest that shouldn't exist.

He stumbled to the nearest trunk, needing to touch it, to prove it was real. The bark felt the same—soft, fibrous, ancient. But wrong. Everything wrong. His fingers found grooves that might have been there yesterday or might have appeared with the impossible winter. In the strange morning light, they looked almost like letters. Almost like words. Almost like warnings written in a language older than writing.

When had he gotten so thin? His hand against the tree looked skeletal, tendons standing out like rope beneath rice-paper skin. He could count his ribs now, feel them shift beneath his shirt with each breath. The forest was hollowing him out, taking pieces of him as payment for... what? For being here? For surviving? For refusing to turn back when turning back was still possible?

If it ever was possible, he thought, and the thought tasted like truth.

His beard—when had he grown a beard?—scratched against his palm as he rubbed his face. Three days of stubble had become something wilder, something that belonged to a man who lived in forests that changed seasons on a whim.

"Okay," he said, addressing the fox, the trees, himself. "Okay. Either I'm losing my mind from starvation, or..." He trailed off. Or what? He had crossed over into another plane of existence entirely? Not just into restricted wilderness but into someplace where October could become December between one breath and the next?

The fox tilted its head—then it stood, shook itself once as if the cold meant nothing, and began walking deeper into the transformed forest.

Micah followed. What else could he do?

Each step crunched on frost that shouldn't exist. His breath clouded the air that had been mild just hours ago. The trees loomed above him, transformed from protective giants into something starker, more honest perhaps.

Without their needles, he could see their true structure—the impossible height, the way they twisted toward a sky that offered no answers.

As he walked, following the fox's red flag through the monochrome morning, Micah began to notice other wrongness. The light fell at angles that hurt to parse, sometimes seeming to come from below, sometimes from all directions at once. Shadows pointed in directions that had nothing to do with where the sun should be. If there was a sun. If such ordinary things as suns and shadows still applied here.

His stomach had stopped growling. That seemed important somehow, that his body had given up on demanding what it couldn't have. He was being pared down to essentials, everything unnecessary stripped away. Fat first, then muscle, then... what? What was left when the physical fell away? What remained when a man was reduced to pure intention, pure will, pure whatever had driven him to walk into a forest that everyone warned him about?

The fox paused at a small rise, looking back with those patient eyes. In the strange light, its fur seemed to shift between red and gold and something that wasn't quite color at all. Real. Still real. The only real thing left.

"I'm coming," Micah whispered, and his voice sounded like wind through bare branches, like winter breathing through hollow bones.

He climbed the rise on legs that felt increasingly theoretical, and at the top, he saw more impossibility waiting. The forest stretched endlessly in all directions, but it was wrong, all wrong. Some trees bare, some in full autumn glory with leaves that shouldn't exist on evergreens, some still green but a green that hurt to look at directly. As if the forest couldn't decide which season to wear, so it wore them all at once.

Micah laughed, or tried to. The sound that emerged was dry as old paper, thin as the air that couldn't seem to fill his lungs properly.

Am I already dead? Is this hell?

As he followed the fox deeper into the forest that couldn't decide what season to be, Micah felt the last threads of his connection to the rational world stretching, stretching, beginning to snap.

The forest had stopped pretending to be normal.

Now it was showing him what it really was.

One moment Micah walked through winter-bare forest, his breath misting in the cold air. The next, autumn leaves crunched beneath his feet. He stopped trying to make sense of it. Sense was a luxury he could no longer afford.

He was following the fox through frost-brittle ferns when the first memory that wasn't his own crashed into him.

Seven years old, learning to ride a bike in the driveway. Concrete hot beneath bare feet, training wheels finally off, his father's hands steady on his shoulders. "You've got this, buddy. I'm right here. I won't let you fall."

Micah stumbled, catching himself against a tree. He remembered this. Except—except he'd learned to ride in the apartment complex parking lot, not a driveway. And his father had been at work, leaving his mother to run alongside him, her encouragement tinged with the exhaustion that never quite left her eyes.

But he could feel the memory like his own. Could taste the orange popsicle melting down his wrist, could hear the neighbor's dog barking, could feel the exact moment when balance clicked into place and the bike became an extension of his body.

His father's memory. Somehow, he was experiencing his father's memory.

Micah pushed forward, and the memories came faster now, flooding through him like water through a broken dam.

Twenty-two years old, standing in Greenwood Cemetery with November rain soaking through his suit. His father's—no, his grandfather's—casket disappearing into the earth. The Purple Heart heavy in his pocket, all that remained of a man who'd left for Korea only to die there. His mother—grandmother?—weeping silent tears while the minister spoke words about sacrifice and service that felt hollow as bird bones.

The memories layered over each other, past and present existing simultaneously. Micah was twenty-one and twenty-two and fifty-two all at once. He was burying his grandfather and being buried by his son and standing at his own grave watching his children—children he'd never had—toss dirt onto wood.

"Stop," he gasped, but the forest wasn't interested in mercy.

Young and terrified, belly-down in mud that might have been Korean or Vietnamese or from some war that hadn't happened yet. His best friend—Thompson? Lee? The name kept changing—bleeding out three feet away, trying to hold his intestines in with fingers that had gone slack. The smell of copper and cordite and human waste. The knowledge settling into his bones: I'm going to carry this forever. It's going to poison everything I touch.

Micah fell to his knees, retching nothing into the frost-touched ferns. He was his grandfather, feeling the exact weight of violence that had taken James in the war. Was his father, inheriting that weight without understanding why his own father stared through walls and flinched at fireworks and drank himself quiet every night. Was himself, carrying all of it forward like some terrible heirloom nobody wanted but everyone received.

The fox approached for the first time since that first night, close enough that Micah could feel its warmth. Real heat from a real creature in this unreal place. It pressed its shoulder against his, and the contact was like a lifeline thrown to a drowning man.

"They didn't mean to," Micah whispered, understanding flooding through him with the borrowed memories. "None of them meant to pass it on."

Another memory: his great-grandfather Harold, younger than Micah was now, staring at the church collection box. Three thousand dollars inside—enough to save his family from the poverty that was killing them by degrees. His hands shaking as he made the choice that would define every generation after. Not just taking the money, but taking it from God's house, knowing he may be caught but not caring.

We're men who steal from God, Micah thought, and didn't know if the thought was his or his father's or Harold's.

The memories kept coming, each one adding another layer to the weight he'd carried without knowing why. His father, thirty-five and exhausted, sitting in his car in the garage with the engine off, just thinking. About how easy it would be to turn the key. About how the pattern was so clear—every man in his line dying young, dying badly. About how maybe it would be kinder to just get it over with before he had a son to pass it on to.

But he'd turned the key the other way. Gone back inside. Kissed his wife. Pretended for another few years that the weight wasn't crushing him.

Micah was sobbing now, great heaving gasps that took all the air the strange forest would give him. Three years since his parents' death and he'd never cried. Had worn his numbness like armor, like strength. But here, experiencing his father's depression from the inside, feeling the exact texture of the despair that had followed Michael Thorne through his days, the tears came like a spring flood.

He cried for his father, who'd carried his own father's war without understanding why he felt like a battlefield. For his grandfather, who'd done terrible necessary things at nineteen and never found a way to put them down. For Harold, whose desperation had cursed his line not with God's wrath but with the knowledge that they were men who took what wasn't theirs.

For himself, the end of the line, carrying all of it and not even knowing why until now.

The fox stayed pressed against him, warm and solid and patient as the trees. The memories began to slow, leaving him gasping on the frozen ground that might not be frozen, beneath trees that couldn't decide what season to wear. He felt emptied out, scoured clean, hollowed as an old bone.

But also, for the first time in his life, he understood.

The men of David's side of the family simply hadn't suffered from the same inherited trauma, passed down like hair color or the shape of a nose. It was his grandfather's violence becoming his father's depression becoming his own blank numbness. It was the weight of what they'd done and what had been done to them, compounding interest through generations.

"We never learned how to put it down," he said to the fox, to the forest, to the ghosts of men who'd died carrying what killed them. "None of us ever learned how to put it down."

The fox stood, shook itself, and looked at him with those ancient eyes. Then it began walking again, deeper into the forest that existed outside of time, outside of season, outside of everything but truth.

Micah followed on legs that barely held him, leaving the puddle of his family's grief frozen in the ferns behind him. He understood now why he'd been called here. Not to die like the others, but to learn what they'd never understood:

Sometimes the only way to break a pattern is to see it clearly, to feel its weight fully, and then to make the choice that all the men before him had been too afraid or too ignorant to make.

The choice to put it down.

The forest path opened before them, leading deeper into whatever trial waited next. But for the first time since entering this impossible place, Micah walked without carrying the full weight of his bloodline's failures.

The visions from the pool still clung to him like water that wouldn't dry.

Micah walked in a kind of daze, his body moving through the motions of following the fox while his mind remained submerged in what he had seen.

He almost walked into the stone.

It rose from the forest floor without warning, a pillar of gray granite that had no business existing in a California redwood forest. Micah stopped short, his hand coming up instinctively to catch himself, and his palm pressed flat against a surface that was surprisingly warm. Not sun-warmed—the canopy here was too dense for direct light—but warm in the way living things were warm.

The fox had stopped a few feet ahead, watching him with those amber eyes that gave nothing away.

Micah pulled his hand back and looked at what stood before him.

The pillar was perhaps eight feet tall, roughly rectangular, its surface covered in carvings that made his breath catch. They were old. Impossibly old. Weathered by centuries of rain and wind that shouldn't have touched them here, beneath the eternal canopy. But more than their age, it was their nature that stopped him.

He recognized them. The angular lines, the interlocking patterns, the figures that were half-human and half-something else. He had seen carvings like these in history books, in documentaries about Viking settlements, in museum exhibits about Norse exploration.

But the Vikings had never reached California. Had never carved their runes into stones that grew warm to the touch in forests that existed outside of time. The wrongness of it—the beautiful, terrible wrongness—made his head swim.

He circled the pillar slowly, studying its faces. Each side bore different markings. The first showed what might have been a tree, a great tree with roots that delved into darkness and branches that reached toward symbols he couldn't interpret. The second depicted figures in procession, their forms stylized but recognizable as human, walking toward something that the carver had rendered as a simple spiral. The third was covered in text, line after line of angular characters that hurt his eyes when he tried to follow them.

The fourth side was blank. Or had been blank. As Micah watched, lines began to appear in the stone. They formed slowly, like frost spreading across glass, creating patterns that seemed to shift and reform even as they solidified.

His hand moved toward the emerging carvings before he could stop it.

The moment his fingers touched the stone, the world inverted. And the carvings moved.

The figures in procession began to walk, their stylized limbs bending and straightening in rhythms that matched no earthly gait. The tree on the first face grew, its roots delving deeper, its branches reaching higher, until it seemed to fill his entire field of vision. The text on the third face rearranged itself, characters sliding across the stone surface like beads on an abacus, forming new configurations that almost— *almost*—resolved into meaning before dissolving again.

The fourth face, the one still forming beneath his touch, showed him something else.

A man. Walking through a forest. Followed by a fox.

The carving was crude, stylized in the same angular fashion as the others, but there was no mistaking what it depicted. The man's posture, hunched with exhaustion. The fox's alert ears, its careful distance. Even the trees around them, rendered in simple lines, captured something essential about this impossible place.

Micah was looking at himself. Carved into stone that was older than America, older than Europe, older than any civilization that had developed the technology to work granite. He was looking at a prophecy or a memory or something that existed outside the distinction between the two.

Below the image, more text formed. Not the angular characters of the other faces, but something his eyes could read even as his mind insisted it was impossible:

The last of his line walks where many have fallen.

He yanked his hand from the stone as if it had burned him.

The world snapped back to its previous configuration—or what passed for normal in a forest that changed seasons between breaths. The carvings were still there, but frozen now, ordinary stone depicting ordinary images. The fourth face had gone blank again, as if the prophecy had never existed.

Micah staggered backward, his breath coming in ragged gasps. His palm tingled where it had touched the granite, a sensation that was half numbness and half electricity. The fox watched him without moving, without offering comfort or guidance. This was something he had to process alone.

"How?" he asked the stone, the fox, the forest, himself. "How is any of this possible?"

No answer came. None was expected. The questions that mattered in this place rarely had answers that could be spoken. They had to be lived.

He circled the pillar again, this time keeping his hands carefully at his sides. The carvings remained static, unchanged, but he could feel them watching him somehow. Feel their weight against his consciousness.

He thought about the words that had formed beneath the image. *The last of his line.* Was that true? He had no children, no siblings, no one to carry the name forward if he failed. If he died here—and the possibility grew more real with each passing hour—the Thorne line would end.

Unless…

The fox made a sound—a soft chirp that drew his attention. It had moved while he was lost in thought, positioning itself at the edge of another path that led deeper into the woods. Time to go. Time to continue the journey.

Micah took one last look at the pillar. In the gray morning light, it looked almost ordinary. But he knew better now.

He followed the fox into the deepening woods, leaving the pillar behind but carrying its message with him.

Micah couldn't feel his feet anymore, but that seemed important in a distant, theoretical way, like remembering he'd once had a phone that needed charging or bills that needed paying. His boots moved beneath him, carrying him forward through a forest that had given up all pretense of following natural law, but the connection between the movement and his consciousness felt increasingly negotiable.

The wrapper of his last granola bar was still in his pocket. The ghost of the memory of his last meal. Silver foil that proved the outside world existed somewhere, even if he could no longer imagine it.

His legs gave out without warning.

One moment he was following the fox through trees that couldn't decide if they were winter-bare or autumn-gold, the next he was on his knees in moss that might have been frosted or might have been starred with tiny flowers. The distinction seemed less important than the fact that he could no longer stand.

"I need—" The words dried up. What did he need? Food, water, rest, home? The concepts felt abstract, like trying to remember the plot of a movie he'd seen years ago.

That's when he saw it. The memorial.

A clearing opened to his left, and in it, arranged with obvious care, were the belongings of those who'd made the same choice he was about to make. Backpacks lined up by size—a child's Disney Princess pack that made his throat close, a military surplus ruck, several REI bags that looked exactly like ones he'd considered buying. Hiking boots in pairs, placed heel to heel like soldiers at attention. A red North Face jacket draped over a fallen log with such precision it looked like the owner had just stepped away for a moment.

Would be right back.

Would never be back.

The fox circled the clearing's edge, not entering. Not letting him enter. But he could see everything he needed to see.

Water bottles still half full. Phones arranged in a line, dark screens reflecting the impossible sky. A child's teddy bear tucked carefully into the crook of a tree. Someone's wedding ring on a flat stone, catching light that had no source.

All of them had reached this point. All of them had decided that whatever the forest offered—oblivion, transformation, reunion with the dead—was better than one more step.

Micah crawled closer, and the fox moved to block him, teeth bared in what wasn't quite a snarl but wasn't encouragement either.

"I could just—" His voice sounded like paper tearing. "Just for a minute. Just rest."

Because that's all it would take. Lie down in that soft moss, close his eyes, let the forest take what it had been trying to take since he'd crossed that first threshold. He could join the neat row of surrendered objects. His wallet next to the others, driver's license face up so someone would know that Micah Thorne had made it this far before choosing to go no farther.

Would anyone even look for him? His landlord would eventually realize the rent wasn't coming. David might wonder why he hadn't returned his calls—oh wait, his phone had died days ago. Sarah might—no, Sarah had already grieved his loss while he was still breathing. She'd been right to leave. He'd been dying by degrees long before he'd entered this forest.

The thought settled over him like a blanket. He'd been dying by degrees his whole life. This would just be making it official.

"Micah."

He jerked upright. Sarah's voice, clear as spring water, coming from the trees beyond the memorial. "Micah, please. This is crazy. You don't have to do this. Just come home."

He knew it wasn't her. Some part of his mind that still functioned properly knew this was the forest offering him what he wanted to hear, showing him the door marked EXIT. But God, it sounded so much like her. Like that last night when she'd begged him to try, to get help, to want something more than the gray existence he'd wrapped around himself like a shroud.

"I can't," he whispered to the voice that wasn't Sarah, to the forest that was listening, to himself. "I don't remember how to want things."

Other voices joined hers. His mother, telling him she'd made his favorite dinner. His father, saying he was proud of him. Carlos from the diner, offering him his job back. Even David, promising that this time would be different, that church wasn't so bad, that there were people who would understand.

All the voices of his abandoned life, calling him back to a world that had never quite felt real even when he was living in it.

The memorial clearing beckoned. Such a simple choice. So many had made it before him. He could see where his body would fit, right there between the military ruck and the designer backpack. The democracy of surrender.

His hands were already moving, pulling off his jacket, when the fox appeared directly in front of him.

Not beside him. Not near him. Directly in his path, those amber eyes blazing with something that wasn't quite anger but was definitely judgment. It had guided him through the forest, led him to water, shown him where to sleep. Now it stood between him and the choice that would end all choices.

"Move," Micah said, but the word had no force behind it.

The fox didn't move.

"I said move!" He tried to shout, but it came out as a whisper. "You don't understand. I'm tired. I'm so fucking tired. I've been tired since before I was born. I inherited tired. I was built out of tired and given a body that doesn't know how to rest."

The fox tilted its head—that gesture he'd come to know so well—but this time it meant something different. Not acknowledgment. Challenge.

You came here for something, those amber eyes seemed to say. *Was it this?*

"Maybe," Micah said, and found he was crying again. When had he become someone who cried? "Maybe that's exactly why I came. Maybe I just needed a place where giving up wouldn't be another failure. Where it would just be... what happens."

The fox stepped closer, close enough that he could see himself reflected in its eyes. What he saw made him look away. Hollow cheeks, wild beard, eyes that had seen too much in too few days. He looked like a ghost already. Maybe that's all he'd ever been. A ghost who'd learned to pretend at living.

But the fox wouldn't let him look away. It pressed its nose against his hand, warm and insistent and absolutely present. The touch said: *You are here. You are now. You are not done yet.*

"I don't know why," Micah whispered, but he found himself standing. Not because he wanted to. Not because he had any hope left. But because the fox was walking away, and after days of following, the habit was stronger than despair.

They left the memorial clearing behind, all those carefully arranged surrenders waiting for the next broken traveler. Micah didn't look back. If he had, he might have seen his jacket on the ground where he'd dropped it, already beginning to fade into the collection.

One foot in front of the other. That's all there was. The fox led, he followed. Through trees that whispered in languages that predated human speech. Past stones arranged in spirals that hurt to perceive. Around pools of water that reflected skies from different seasons, different worlds.

The voices followed for a while—Sarah, his parents, everyone he'd failed or who'd failed him—but eventually they faded too. Even hallucinations required energy, and he had none left to spare.

The forest path wound upward, though there was no mountain he could remember. The trees grew older, larger, more impossible. Some had faces in their bark that might have been carved or might have been grown. Some bled sap that looked too much like tears. Some stood in formations that suggested architecture, as if someone had been building a cathedral out of living wood and forgotten to finish it.

When they finally stopped, the sun—or whatever passed for the sun in this place—was setting. Or rising. The light had the quality of transition, though from what to what, Micah couldn't say.

The fox sat at the edge of another clearing, but this one was different. No memorials here. No surrendered belongings. Just a circle of stones, each one carved with symbols that seemed to swim and shift when he tried to focus on them. The space inside the circle felt expectant, like a held breath.

"What now?" Micah asked the fox, the forest, himself. "Another test? Another memory? Another chance to give up?"

The fox entered the circle and looked back at him. Waiting.

Micah understood without understanding. This was a threshold. Another one. How many more could there be? How many times could a person choose to keep going before the choices ran out?

He entered the circle.

The moment his foot crossed the boundary, the exhaustion hit him like a physical weight. Not the bone-deep tiredness he'd been carrying, but something older and heavier. The exhaustion of his entire bloodline, generations of men who'd carried what they couldn't name until it crushed them.

But this time, kneeling in the circle of ancient stones, Micah did something none of them had ever done.

He set it down.

Not the exhaustion—that was his to carry a little longer. But the certainty that it would kill him. The inheritance of early death. The conviction that he was destined to repeat the pattern.

***

The forest had changed its mind about something.

Micah felt the shift before he saw it, a subtle alteration in the air pressure, in the way sound moved between the trees. He'd been following the fox through the aftermath of his collapse, each step an act of will, when suddenly the path ahead cleared. Not gradually, the way trails sometimes revealed themselves through undergrowth, but deliberately.

For the first time since passing the warning sign, he stood on something that could only be called a road.

Stones had been placed at intervals, each one flat and broad enough to serve as a stepping stone. They were carved with symbols that made his eyes water if he looked directly at them, but he found he could perceive them sideways, the way you might catch a faint star in your peripheral vision. The symbols whispered meanings just below the threshold of understanding: *approach, prepare, be worthy, be judged.*

The fox walked this path differently. Gone was the cautious guide who'd kept its distance, who'd led him to water and shelter with the wariness of a wild thing. This fox moved with ceremony, placing each paw precisely on the carved stones. Its red coat seemed brighter in the twilight, more flame than fur.

"Where are we going?" Micah asked, though he didn't expect an answer. His voice sounded strange to his own ears—hoarse from disuse, yes, but also different in pitch, as if the forest had been slowly retuning him like an instrument.

The trees along this path were the oldest he'd seen yet. Not just ancient but primordial, their trunks so vast that they felt like canyon walls. Some had grown together over millennia, fusing into structures that defied classification as single or multiple organisms. Their bark showed patterns that looked deliberate—whorls and spirals that reminded him of the stone circles, of Celtic knots, of diagrams he'd seen in physics textbooks about the shape of spacetime.

These trees had been here before his species learned to dream. Would be here after his species forgot how to wake. They leaned over the path not with menace but with attention, as if noting his passage in whatever way trees note things.

As they climbed—and they were climbing, though he couldn't remember when the ground had begun to slope— Micah noticed other signs of intention in the landscape. Stone cairns appeared at regular intervals, each one built with a precision that spoke of ritual rather than mere trail marking. Some of the stones were natural, worn smooth by ages of water and wind. Others were carved with those same swimming symbols, or with faces that might have been human once, before time softened their features into suggestion.

The fog that had been his constant companion since entering the forest began to behave differently here. Instead of clinging to everything, obscuring and confusing, it moved in patterns. Streams of mist flowed along specific routes, revealing certain trees while concealing others. Opening views of the path ahead just far enough to show the next few steps, then closing like curtains.

They passed between two trees that could only be described as a gateway. Not carved, not shaped by human hands, but grown over centuries into an arch so perfect it made his chest ache. The moment he walked beneath it, the temperature changed. Warmer, despite the evening hour. The air smelled different too—less pine and earth, more herbs and smoke and something floral he couldn't name.

Beyond the gateway, the path widened into what could only be called a road. Still unpaved, but worn smooth by the passage of... what? Not feet like his. The wear patterns were wrong for human traffic. This was a road used by things that moved differently, that had different relationships with the ground.

His body, pushed beyond exhaustion into some strange state of clarity, moved without his conscious direction. One foot in front of the other, following the fox, following the path, following whatever thread had been pulling him since he'd first dreamed of this forest. The hunger had passed through pain into a kind of emptiness that felt almost peaceful. His thoughts moved strangely, sometimes racing, sometimes crawling, always circling back to a single question: What was he being prepared for?

The trees grew impossibly larger. He passed one whose trunk would have taken fifty people holding hands to encircle. Its bark was marked with what looked like handprints—hundreds of them, pressed into the living wood at different heights, from different eras. Some were clearly ancient, worn nearly smooth. Others looked fresh enough that he expected to find the person who'd made them waiting around the next bend.

Were they marks of passage? Promises? Warnings? He raised his own hand toward the trunk, then stopped. Whatever ritual this represented, he hadn't earned the right to participate. Not yet.

The fox watched this moment of restraint with what Micah was beginning to recognize as approval. Then it continued up the path, and he followed, leaving the marked tree and its mysterious testimonies behind.

The light was definitely changing now, not just in intensity but in quality. The amber glow that had suffused the forest since he'd entered was deepening, becoming richer, more golden, like honey held up to flame. It made everything look ancient and precious and slightly unreal. Or maybe more real. Maybe this was how the world actually looked when you scraped away all the modern noise and distraction.

They crested in a final rise, and Micah had to stop, relieved to see a quiet grove, one tailor made for him to make camp.

The fire should have been impossible to build.

Micah's hands shook too badly to strike the matches properly, and the wood he'd gathered was damp with fog that seemed to generate from the earth itself. But something wanted this fire to exist. It took several tries, but finally, the matches caught. The kindling took the flame like it had been waiting for it. Within minutes, he had a blaze that pushed back the darkness and painted the grove's edge in dancing shadows.

The fox settled closer than it ever had before, just within the circle of warmth, its red fur turned copper by the flames. Not touching—they'd only touched twice in all these days, both times when Micah had been breaking apart—but near enough that he could have reached out if he chose. He didn't. Some distances were important to maintain, especially here at the edge of... whatever this was.

For the first time since entering the forest, the supernatural activity that had been his constant companion—the whispers, the shadows, the sense of being watched—went quiet. The forest that had spent days testing and tormenting him now offered something like peace.

His mind, scoured clean by exhaustion and revelation, couldn't hold onto thoughts or plans for what tomorrow would bring. Instead, he found himself simply existing. Watching the fire. Feeling the warmth. Being present in his body despite how little body there seemed to be left.

The stars above were visible through breaks in the canopy, and for once they looked right. Familiar constellations in their proper places—Orion's belt, the Big Dipper, Polaris holding steady in the north. As if the forest was allowing him this one comfort, this reminder that somewhere beyond the trees, the ordinary world continued its ordinary business.

"My father never saw stars like this," Micah said to the fox, to the fire, to himself. "Too much light pollution where we lived. He always talked about taking me camping, showing me the real night sky. Never got around to it."

The fox's ear twitched, but it didn't open its eyes. Listening but not responding, maintaining its role as witness rather than participant.

"I used to be angry about that. All the things he said we'd do but never did. Now I understand he was too tired. Carrying what he carried, just getting through each day was an accomplishment." Micah fed another stick to the fire, watched the sparks rise toward those impossible stars.

"I forgive him. For all of it. The distance, the drinking, the dying. None of it was about me."

The words felt like stones leaving his chest, each one making breathing easier. He'd carried that anger so long it had become part of his architecture. Without it, he felt strangely hollow. Clean but empty, like a house after all the furniture has been removed.

The fox cracked one amber eye, regarded him for a moment, then closed it again. Approval or dismissal, Micah couldn't tell. Maybe it didn't matter.

The fire burned lower, and he didn't feed it. Some vigils required darkness. As the flames died to coals, the grove beyond became more visible, lit by starlight and something else, some quality of the trees themselves that suggested rather than showed. He could make out the patterns now—the circles within circles, the way each tree stood in perfect relation to all the others. It was mathematics made manifest, geometry given root and bark and reaching branches.

No wind stirred the canopy. No night birds called. Even the omnipresent fog had withdrawn, leaving the air clear and still as held breath. The forest waited with him, keeping vigil for whatever transformation dawn would bring.

He lay down beside the dying fire, and the fox—in a gesture that broke all its careful rules—curled against his back. Warm. Solid. Real.

Sleep took him between one breath and the next, and for the first time since entering the forest, he dreamed nothing at all. No visions. No visitors. No memories that weren't his own. Just the deep, healing darkness that comes after the work is done and before the judgment begins.

Micah woke to sunlight that shouldn't exist.

Real sun, not the ambient glow that had lit the forest since his arrival, poured through the canopy in thick golden shafts. It painted the grove in colors he'd forgotten were possible—true green, rich brown, the silver of morning mist burning off bark. After days of twilight, the brightness made his eyes water.

The fox stood at the clearing's edge, silhouetted against this impossible dawn. Its coat blazed red-gold in the morning light, and when it looked back at him, those amber eyes held something new. Not farewell—not yet—but acknowledgment that their journey together was entering its final phase.

Every muscle screamed as Micah pushed himself upright. His body was a catalog of deprivation—ribs like ladder rungs, skin stretched tight over vanishing muscle, hands that trembled with weakness. But his mind was clear. Clearer than it had been in years, maybe clearer than it had ever been. The fog that had shrouded his thoughts since his parents' death had burned away, leaving him raw but present.

He stood slowly, joints protesting, and looked toward the grove's heart where answers waited. Or questions. Or judgment. Or transformation. Or death.

He wasn't afraid.

"Today," he said to the fox, and it dipped its head once in agreement.

Today, he would learn why he'd been called here. Today, he would face whatever his ancestors had fled from or toward. Today, the pattern would either break or claim its final victim.

CHAPTER 7:
THE ANCIENT GAME

Micah was a ghost of the man who'd entered the forest. His jeans hung loose on hips that were all bone now, held up only by the belt he'd tightened to its last notch yesterday… or the day before. His hands shook from hunger, but his mind remained clear. As if the comfortable lies he'd told himself had burned away with what little excess body fat he'd carried. Now only what was essential remained.

The fox led him along a path that was no longer ambiguous. Stones had been placed at deliberate intervals, each one flat and broad enough to serve as a stepping stone. They were carved with symbols that made his eyes water if he looked directly at them, but he somehow understood them, catching their meaning in peripheral glances: *approach, prepare, be worthy, be judged.*

This was a road. Others had walked it. Maybe all those the forest had claimed had walked it, each in their own time, each failing or fleeing before reaching its end.

But Micah would reach it. He had to. There was nowhere else to go, nothing else to be done. Forward was the only direction that existed anymore. The road seemed to pull him forward, compelling him to continue. The trees here stood apart from each other like sentinels at their posts, their spacing regular instead of the chaotic twisting and swirling of the previous chaotic forest. Between their trunks, shadows gathered with unnatural density, creating walls of darkness that made the path feel like a salvation, the only thing the light could touch.

The air grew heavy as he walked, pressing against him with almost physical weight. The fox's red coat stood as the only warm color in a landscape drained of life by the approaching dusk. Every few steps it would pause and look back, not checking if he followed but more like ensuring he was prepared for what lay ahead.

Something in the forest's silence had changed. Not the mere absence of sound he'd grown accustomed to, but an active quiet, as if the trees themselves were holding their breath. The temperature dropped steadily, and Micah felt his skin prickle with awareness of being watched by more than bark and leaves. This was approach to sacred ground, to a place where the forest's power concentrated. His body, worn to nothing but will and forward motion, recognized the nearness of ending.

The sun was beginning its descent when they crested a final rise. Below lay a clearing that could have been designed by ancient mathematicians. A perfect circle. Ancient redwoods standing as sentinels around a space where no tree had ever grown, grass short as if maintained by invisible hands.

In the center, a fire pit made of stones so old they'd worn smooth, arranged in a spiral pattern that pulled the eye inward, demanding attention and offering no escape from its geometric perfection.

The fox sat at the clearing's edge and looked at Micah, then at the fire pit, then back at Micah.

This is where you wait. This is where it happens.

Understanding the silent message, Micah descended into the clearing, each step a negotiation with muscles that had been eating themselves for days. But he made it to the center, to the ancient fire pit.

He gathered wood with shaking hands, built the fire with the methodical care his father had taught him a lifetime ago. The familiar motions grounded him—kindling nest, graduated sizes, leaving space for air to flow. His father's matches were down to their last few, but they'd gotten him this far. One caught on the first strike, as if the universe was conserving his resources for him now.

Night was coming. Real night. And with it...

He didn't know what. But he was ready.

Micah fed the fire carefully, building it strong but not wasteful. He had no food left, but a distant part of him remembered that people sometimes fasted for clarity… to help them listen for something greater. Maybe he shouldn't have brought food at all.

The first stars appeared in a sky that actually darkened properly, fading from gold to rose to deep purple to black.

The stars glowed from their normal positions, just as they had last night. Orion rising in the east, the Dipper wheeling around Polaris. After days of impossible skies, the normalcy was almost more unsettling than the strangeness had been.

That's when he noticed the mushrooms.

They grew in a perfect ring around the fire pit, just at the edge where firelight met darkness. Golden caps that seemed to glow with their own inner light, the same ones the fox had led him to days ago. He understood without understanding: these were meant for now. For tonight. For whatever was coming.

Micah picked three—the number felt right—and ate them slowly, thoughtfully. They tasted of earth and autumn and, somehow, home.

The mushrooms' effects crept through him slowly, gently. Far from the violent upheaval he'd seen illustrated on tv shows, there was only a subtle shifting of his perception. Colors in the firelight deepened, bringing forth hues he'd never noticed: blues hidden in the orange, purples dancing at the edges of flame. Time stretched like honey, each crackling spark from the fire hanging in the air long enough to trace its path.

Micah sat in perfect stillness, aware of his heartbeat syncing with some deeper rhythm—the forest's pulse, perhaps, or the earth's slow breathing beneath him. The boundary between his body and the ground he sat on grew soft, negotiable. He was here, in this clearing, but also somehow part of it, woven into the same fabric as the trees and stones and watching stars. He could not tell how long he sat there, nor did he care. He existed in a moment that was all moments, waiting without impatience for whatever the night would bring.

The fox's ears pricked forward. Its attention shifted from Micah to the darkness beyond the firelight.

He looked up from the fire to see a woman emerge from the darkness between two ancient redwoods, and his breath caught.

Impossibly old. That was his first thought. Beyond ancient. She looked like she'd already been old when this forest was young, when the very stones of the fire pit were first arranged. Her face was a map of wrinkles so deep they seemed to hold stories, secrets, the memory of ages.

Forest creature, was the phrase echoing in Micah's head, his memory grasping at old fairy tales his mother had told him as a child. Whatever this woman was—real or hallucination—she was not human. Not the way Micah was, anyway.

She wore a dark cloak heavy with adornments—beads of wood and bone, crystals that caught firelight and threw it back in colors that had no names, small pouches of leather so old it had blackened. Her white hair was long, braided with strips of bark and threaded with what might have been moss or might have been something else entirely. At her belt hung a larger pouch that seemed to pulse with its own subtle rhythm.

Her eyes, when they fixed on Micah, were the only young thing about her. Dark but alive with an intelligence that made him want to look away and stare at the same time.

"Micah Thorne," she said, and her voice was wind through caves, water over stone, the forest speaking with human tongue. "Last of your line."

She moved with deliberate grace, circling the fire pit to sit across from him. Despite her apparent age, she folded herself to the ground with the fluid ease of someone who had never known the betrayal of joints and bones. The firelight loved her, painting her weathered face in gold and shadow, making the crystals on her cloak spark like captured stars.

The fox approached her, and she touched its head with a tenderness that made Micah's throat close. Here was recognition, old friendship, a bond that predated his arrival by years or decades or more.

"My old friend has brought you far," she said to the fox, then looked back at Micah. "Through trials that break most men. You have done well to reach this place."

"What is this place?" Micah's voice was hoarse, barely recognizable as his own.

"The threshold. Where debts are paid or carried forward." She pulled a small clay cup from her cloak, seemingly from nowhere, and filled it from a waterskin that appeared with the same impossible ease. The liquid that poured was dark, herbal, aromatic enough to reach him across the fire. "Most have failed. Turned back at the grove of eyes. Lost themselves in the pool of mirrors. Succumbed to the memorial clearing's permanent peace. But you..."

She held the cup out across the flames. "You are here. Hollowed out, burned clean, ready to see clearly. Drink. What comes next requires vision beyond sight, and you have been too long walking between worlds. The herbs will help you see truly."

Micah accepted the cup with hands that shook not from fear but from simple physical weakness. The liquid was warm, though it couldn't have been heated. It tasted of mushroom and bark, of midnight rain and morning dew, of green things growing in darkness. As he drank, the edges of the world grew both sharper and softer, as if reality was coming into focus while simultaneously revealing its fluid nature.

"I am Eldrazi," she said as he finished the cup. "Keeper of thresholds, holder of games, judge of hearts. I have waited here since before your people gave names to their sins. I am the forest's memory and its justice, its mercy and its hunger."

She reached into her belt pouch and pulled out something that made Micah's breath catch. A wooden board, ancient and dark with age, carved with cup-like depressions. A game board. And from another impossible fold in her cloak, a leather bag that rattled with the sound of stones.

"And you are here," Eldrazi said, placing the board on the ground between them with ceremonial care. "Here, in these deep woods, where we will take your measure. You have earned the right to play."

"What am I playing for?" Micah asked, though he thought he already knew.

"A chance," Eldrazi said simply. "One game. One opportunity to enter the spirit world that always moves through and around you. Undetected but there all the same. Win, and you may break free of what binds your blood. Lose..."

She didn't need to finish. Micah had seen the memorial clearing, all those carefully arranged belongings. He knew what happened to those who played the ancient games and lost.

"What's the game?" he asked, though that too was becoming clear as she positioned the board with precise care.

"Mancala," she said, and pulled the stones from their bag. They spilled across her palm like drops of night—obsidian, fathomless as the spaces between stars, smooth as water, heavy with more than physical weight. "A game older than chess, older than war. A game of patterns and patience, of knowing when to give and when to take. Fitting, for one who seeks to break patterns generations in the making."

She began placing the stones in the cups, six to each hollow, her movements ritualistic and exact. The click of stone on wood sounded louder than it should, echoing in spaces that existed beyond the merely physical.

"You may refuse," Eldrazi said as she placed the last stone. "Turn back now. Return to your life, your apartment, your slow familiar dying. Many do, when they understand the stakes. There is no shame in choosing known suffering over unknown risk."

Micah looked at the board, at the stones that seemed to swallow light, at his hands that shook with exhaustion and hunger and the weight of everything he'd carried to reach this moment. He thought of his father. His grandfather. All the Thorne men, crushed under the weight of inherited doom.

He thought of David, thriving, protected by something Micah had been too proud to accept. And he thought of the son he might someday have, who would carry this forward if Micah failed tonight.

Above them, the moon broke through the canopy—full, silver, impossibly large. Its light joined with the firelight to illuminate the board, making the obsidian stones gleam like dark mirrors. The fox opened its eyes fully, watching. Eldrazi waited with the patience of ages.

"I'll play," Micah said.

She smiled, and it was terrible and beautiful and ancient as the forest itself. "Then let us see if you are the one who breaks the pattern, or if the pattern breaks you. The moon is witness. The forest is judge. The game begins."

She gestured to the board, its cups waiting like small graves, like possibilities, like doors that could open into freedom or finality.

Micah's hand hovered over the board, but before he could select his first cup, Eldrazi raised her own hand—a gesture that carried the weight of command despite its gentleness.

"Not yet," she said. "First, you must understand fully what you play for. Knowledge incomplete is worse than ignorance. You know pieces of your family's story, fragments glimpsed in fever dreams and borrowed memories. But the whole truth—that, you deserve to see before you choose your path across this board."

She passed her hand over the fire, and the flames responded like trained animals, leaping higher, changing color from orange to deep blue to something that had no name. In the heart of the fire, images began to form—not vague suggestions but clear as life, as if Micah was looking through a window into the past.

Salem. October, 1692. But not the Salem of popular imagination with its pointed hats and cartoon witches. This was a real place full of real people, mud streets and timber houses, fear thick as morning fog. The trial was already underway when the vision focused, showing a packed courthouse where neighbors turned against neighbors for spite or sport or profit.

"Watch closely," Eldrazi commanded. "See your beginning."

Ezekiel Thorne stood in the witness box. Only slightly older than Micah was now—maybe twenty-five—with the kind of austere handsomeness that marked him as righteous in the eyes of his community. This was not a face or a name Micah had seen in his mother's box of tragic memories. A long-dead ancestor who should have been a stranger was somehow as real and familiar to him as his own father.

Ezekiel's clothes were well-made, his bearing confident. A man on the rise, with a new wife and new land and new status in the colony.

In the defendant's chair sat the woman wearing simple gray, her dark hair bound severely back, her hands folded calmly despite the chains. Her eyes, when they fixed on Ezekiel, held disappointment deeper than fear.

"Rebecca Morse. She had saved his infant son not three months prior," Eldrazi narrated as the vision played out. "The child—your ancestor—burned with fever. The physician had given up, told Ezekiel to prepare for burial. Rebecca came unbidden, worked through the night with herbs and songs older than Christ's cross. By morning, the baby lived."

In the fire, Ezekiel's testimony unfolded with damning clarity. He spoke of seeing Rebecca gathering herbs by moonlight. Of strange lights in her cottage windows. Of cats that followed her, of crows that brought her messages. Each word carefully chosen to damn without outright lying, to suggest without stating, to let the court's fear fill in the gaps.

"He owed her his son's life," Eldrazi continued, her voice heavy with old anger. "She had asked nothing in return. 'Healing is its own reward,' she'd told him. But her land abutted his. Good bottom land, perfect for planting. And the colony had made clear that the property of condemned witches would be redistributed to faithful citizens."

When Rebecca finally spoke, her voice was clear, carrying despite the crowd's hostile murmurs.

"I have healed your children and eased your elders' passing. I have asked nothing but to live quietly, hurting none. If this is witchcraft, then Christ himself was a witch, for did he not heal with touch and word?"

The gallery erupted. Blasphemy added to witchcraft. Ezekiel's face showed a moment's doubt—just a flicker—before hardening back into righteous certainty. He had committed to this course. Too late to turn back now.

"See how doubt entered him," Eldrazi said. "See how he pushed it down. Every curse needs such a moment—when truth is recognized and refused. That refusal becomes the crack through which darkness enters."

The trial proceeded with foregone conclusion. Other witnesses, other lies, building a wall of fear around a woman whose only crime was knowledge and independence. When the sentence came—death by hanging—Rebecca received it with the same calm she'd shown throughout.

But as they led her out, she stopped before Ezekiel. The guards tried to pull her along, but she stood rooted as an oak, and her voice when she spoke carried to every corner of the courthouse.

"Ezekiel Thorne," she said, and her tone was not angry but sorrowful. "You have killed the one who saved your son. You have stolen from the one who gave freely. You have borne false witness for gain and wrapped greed in God's name."

The crowd had gone silent, even her accusers struck dumb by the power in her voice. She wasn't ranting or railing. She was simply stating facts, and everyone present knew them to be true.

"Hear then the fruit of your planting," Rebecca continued. "The sons of your line will know the weight you have put upon me. They will carry what you have stolen. They will die as I die—young, unjustly, with work unfinished."

She looked past Ezekiel then, her eyes unfocusing as if seeing through time itself. "But know this—grace remains for those who seek it. Faith truly held breaks all chains. The curse cannot cling where God's hand rests."

The guards pulled her toward the door, but she turned back one final time. "I forgive you, Ezekiel Thorne. But forgiveness does not erase consequence. You have sown. Your sons will reap."

The vision shifted to the hanging tree. The crowd gathered, expectant. The noose prepared. Rebecca standing calm as still water while prayers were read and charges recited. But as the trap prepared to drop, as Ezekiel watched from the front row already thinking of which fields he'd plant first—

She vanished.

No flash. No smoke. No drama. Simply there one moment, gone the next. The empty noose swung in the wind while the crowd erupted in panic, in terror, in validation of their fears. A real witch. They had caught and tried and almost executed a real witch.

The fire's vision faded, returning to normal flames. Micah sat stunned, the full weight of his family's origin settling into his bones. Not a vague curse from an angry woman, but specific consequences for specific sins. Theft. False witness. Murder wrapped in righteousness.

"She survived?" he asked.

"She fled," Eldrazi corrected. "West, always west, staying ahead of rumors and accusations. She was young then, heartbroken by the betrayal of those she'd helped. She used her arts only to hide after that, to disappear, to become nobody and nothing. I found her decades later, aged beyond her years, power turned inward like a blade. She died quietly, unknown, unmourned except by me."

"And the curse held."

"Words spoken at such extremity carry their own life. She could no more have called it back than you could call back a stone once thrown. It settled into your bloodline like water into a waiting vessel." Eldrazi's ancient eyes studied him. "Tell me what you see in your family's pattern."

Micah thought of all he'd learned, all he'd experienced in these impossible days. "Early death, always. But more than that. We're... broken with faith. Can't hold it. My great-grandfather stole from churches. My grandfather found no God in war. My father couldn't pray even when he wanted to. And me..."

"And you?"

"I turned away every chance I got. Like something in my blood recognized churches as enemy territory." Understanding dawned like cold sunlight. "We became what Ezekiel pretended to be—Godless men. The very thing he accused Rebecca of being, we became."

"The curse is elegant in its justice," Eldrazi agreed. "He wore faith like a mask to hide greed, so his sons would find no mask would fit."

"But David—"

"Ah, David." Eldrazi smiled, and it was less terrible this time, almost fond. "Tell me of the moment when your lines divided."

Micah had to think. His mother's genealogy work, the family trees she'd carefully mapped. "David's great-great-grandfather. Josiah Thorne's younger brother, Marcus. He... he was different."

The fire flared again, showing another vision. Two young men in 1850s California. Josiah—Micah's direct ancestor—planning another religious con, another traveling preacher scam. Marcus refusing to participate. An argument. A split.

"I won't wear God as a disguise anymore," Marcus said in the vision. "I won't follow you down this path, brother. What we do—what our father did, what his father did—it's wrong. It's all wrong."

"See how one brother chose differently," Eldrazi said as the vision showed Marcus walking away, leaving behind family and the easy money of religious fraud. "He joined a small congregation. Confessed his family's sins. Worked honestly. Raised his children in genuine faith. Not perfect faith—perfection isn't required—but sincere. Real."

The vision shifted through generations. David's line, marked by their own struggles but held steady by that genuine faith passed down like heirloom seeds. They had their failures, their doubts, their dark nights, but they never let go of that fundamental connection Marcus had fought to reclaim.

"So simple," Micah said, understanding flooding through him. "One brother chose to stop running from God. That's all. That's the only difference between David and me—somewhere back in our family tree, his line turned toward what mine kept running from."

"Simple to say," Eldrazi corrected. "Harder to do. He walks with God. Even as you do not."

Micah felt tears on his face, hot in the cool night air. His throat twisted, choking off the angry retort forming on his lips. *I'm a good person! I always tried to do the right thing! You don't know me!*

The sad string of defensive platitudes fell flat even in his own mind. Weren't those the words of every failure? Every criminal and charlatan? They all said the same thing when confronted with their inequity because the elixir of truth tasted too foul to swallow.

All the Thorne men had run from this simple truth. But here, at the fire, the flames flickering in the Eldrazi's ancient eyes, Micah could not run as his forbears had.

She gestured to the board between them. "You have seen truly these past days—your family's history, your own heart, the weight you've carried. You have put down what wasn't yours in the grove of eyes. Now comes the game, and only your heart knows if it is honest."

"What happens if I lose?"

Eldrazi's expression was neither kind nor cruel, simply factual. "You remain here. Part of the forest, like those whose belongings you saw in the memorial clearing. Not dead, not alive. Suspended. Your line ended, yet the curse unbroken."

"And if I win?"

"Then you return to the world freed. The curse dies with the dawn. Your children—all the future children of your line—born into clean air, able to choose their own paths without inherited weight." She tilted her head, studying him. "But winning isn't about skill at Mancala. The game is older than its rules. It reads hearts, not strategies. It knows honest from false, courage from bravado, acceptance from resignation."

Micah looked at the board. Such a simple thing. Wood and cups and stones. But in this place, with this woman, under this moon, it was also judgment and jury and the weight of generations.

"My father," Micah said suddenly. "That day in the garage. He was so close to..."

"To ending it badly, yes. As his father considered in Korea. As Harold considered before fleeing west. Each generation faced that moment when the weight seemed unbearable." Eldrazi's voice held compassion now. "But each chose to carry it forward instead. Perhaps that too was courage, in its way. Choosing the harder path of continued suffering rather than the escape of self-destruction."

"Or maybe they were just cowards," Micah said bitterly.

"Or perhaps they hoped, without knowing they hoped, that one day a son would come who could do what they couldn't. Who would walk into the deep woods and face the truth and play the game with honest heart." She gestured to the space around them. "You are here. They are not. Draw what conclusions you will."

The moon had risen higher, its light falling directly into the clearing now. The perfect circle of trees, the ancient fire pit, the game board waiting—everything aligned for this moment that had been generations in the making.

"I need to know," Micah said. "The mushrooms, the tea—am I drugged? Is any of this real?"

Eldrazi laughed, that bone-chime sound. "What is real? Is your hunger real? Yes. Is your exhaustion real? Yes. Is the curse that has killed your fathers real? You have lived its reality. Are the visions I show you real? They are true, which is better than real. Is this game real?" She touched the board with one gnarled finger. "Real enough to save or damn you."

"That's not an answer."

"It is the only answer that matters. You sought the deep woods. You found them. Whether they exist in the world of maps and satellites or only in the world of souls—what difference does that make to you, here, now?"

She was right. Micah had passed beyond caring about consensus reality somewhere around the time the forest changed seasons overnight. What mattered was what happened next. What mattered was the choice to play or flee.

The moon watched. The fox watched. The forest itself seemed to lean in, ancient trees pressing closer to witness this moment they had been waiting for since Ezekiel Thorne first pointed a lying finger at an innocent woman.

"Are you ready?" Eldrazi asked.

Micah looked at his hands—thin now, worn down to essential bone and sinew. He thought of all the hands before his that should have held these stones. All the chances missed, the patterns repeated, the weight carried forward.

"I'm ready," he said.

The stones sat in their cups like drops of condensed night, forty-eight pieces of obsidian that seemed to pull light into themselves rather than reflect it. Eldrazi had finished explaining the basic rules—how each player controlled the six cups on their side, how stones moved counterclockwise, how capturing worked when your final stone landed in an empty cup. Simple rules that every child learned, that existed in variations across every culture that had discovered the satisfaction of dropping stones into waiting hollows.

But as Micah studied the board, he understood that this was no children's game. The wood itself seemed alive under his fingers, warm with more than reflected firelight. The cups weren't simply depressions carved into timber—they were perfectly formed spirals that drew the eye inward, each one unique yet part of a greater pattern that spoke of mathematics beyond human comprehension. And the stones...

"These aren't ordinary obsidian," he said, picking one up. It was heavier than it should be, and perfectly smooth, as if polished by centuries of handling. Yet when he looked closely, he could see things moving within its depths—stars, perhaps, or the memory of stars.

"Nothing here is ordinary," Eldrazi replied. "This board was already ancient when your people learned to count the objects they would someday drop into it. These stones were gathered from places where the world grows thin, where what is and what might be touch briefly before parting ways." She lifted one of her own stones, holding it to the firelight. "In another age, men would have called them sacred. Now they are just stones. Both truths are equally correct."

Micah set the stone back in its cup, the soft click echoing in the clearing's perfect acoustics. "When you say winning isn't about skill…"

"I say that because it is true. The game plays you as much as you play it. Each move reveals character. Each choice shows the shape of your soul. Patient or impulsive. Generous or grasping. Thinking only of victory or considering the beauty of the patterns you create." She touched her side of the board. "I have played this game with dying children who won because their hearts were pure. I have played with master strategists who lost because their hearts were hollow. Skill helps, but spirit decides."

The fox, which had been silent and still as a statue, suddenly stretched and padded closer to the fire. It settled again equally distant from both players, a witness rather than ally. Its amber eyes caught the moonlight and held it, becoming two small moons of their own.

"What about you?" Micah asked suddenly. "What do you get out of this? Why sit here, generation after generation, playing games with cursed men?"

Eldrazi smiled, and for a moment looked almost human. Almost young. "What makes you think I have a choice? I am as bound to this role as you are to your bloodline's debt. I serve my purpose as you serve yours. The difference is, I have made peace with my purpose. You still fight yours."

The fire crackled, sending sparks up toward the watching stars. One landed on the board between them, glowing for a moment before going dark. Eldrazi brushed the ash away with careful fingers.

"Can the game end in a draw?"

"No. One wins, one loses. The board itself will ensure this—if we reach a position where continuation is impossible, it will declare a victor by methods I cannot predict. The game wants resolution. It hungers for endings, one way or another."

Micah absorbed this, feeling the weight of it settle onto his shoulders alongside everything else he carried. Then a thought struck him. "How many games have you played?"

"More than there are stones on this board. More than there are trees in this grove." Her voice held the weariness of ages. "I have watched the hopeful and the hopeless, the guilty and the innocent, the wise and the foolish. I have seen every possible way to win and every possible way to lose. Yet each game surprises me. Each player brings something new to these ancient patterns."

"Do you ever let them win?"

Her eyes flashed with something that might have been anger or might have been respect. "The game cannot be given. Victory cannot be gifted. To try would be to corrupt the very thing that grants it power. I play honestly, always. I play to win, always. To do otherwise would be to insult you, the forest, and the purpose we serve."

"Good," Micah said, and meant it. "I don't want charity. I want truth."

"Then truth you shall have." She reached into her pouch again and withdrew something else—a small hourglass, no bigger than her palm. The sand inside was silver, flowing upward instead of down. "We play until this runs its course. If neither has won by then, whoever holds more stones claims victory. Another fairness—time limits prevent the game from becoming eternal stalemate."

"How long?"

"As long as it needs to be. The glass knows. It measures more than mortal hours." She placed it beside the board, but did not yet turn it. "Any other questions? Any other fears to voice? Once we begin, we play to completion."

Micah looked at his hands again. The tremor had stopped sometime during their conversation, replaced by a strange steadiness. His body was failing—he could feel that in every movement—but his spirit felt clearer than it had since childhood. Before the weight settled. Before he understood what it meant to be a Thorne man.

"My ancestor," he said. "Ezekiel. Did he ever know what he'd done? Did the curse touch him?"

"He prospered," Eldrazi said simply. "Died old and rich, surrounded by children who sang hymns at his bedside. But yes, he knew. The knowing was his only punishment—to see his son grow strange and distant, to watch the boy struggle with faith like a man trying to wear clothes that don't fit. To realize, too late, that some thefts can never be returned, some lies can never be untold. He died begging God's forgiveness. Whether he received it is between him and his Maker."

The moon had reached its apex, hanging directly overhead like a cosmic eye. The shadows in the clearing had shrunk to nothing, everything bathed in silver-white radiance that made the ordinary world seem like a half-remembered dream. Even the fire looked different in this light, its flames more silver than gold.

"I'm ready," Micah said, and found it was true. Whatever happened next, he'd earned his place at this board. The trials had prepared him—not to win, necessarily, but to play with honest heart. To meet his fate with eyes open.

The forest itself seemed to hold its breath, ancient trees leaning in to witness this moment they'd waited centuries to see.

"Choose your first cup," Eldrazi said, hand poised on the hourglass. "Make your first move. Show the board who you are."

Micah studied the six cups on his side, each holding four stones. Twenty-four pieces of captive night, waiting to be released into motion. Such a simple game. Such impossible stakes. His hand moved toward the rightmost cup. The stones were warm, almost alive under his touch. Waiting to begin their journey around the board, carrying his hopes and fears with them.

Eldrazi turned the hourglass. Silver sand began its impossible upward flow.

"Then play, Micah Thorne," she said formally. "Play for your freedom. Play for your bloodline. Play for all the sons who will come after, born free or born weighted. Play with honest heart, and let the pattern finally find its ending."

Micah lifted the four stones from the cup, feeling their weight. Then, with a deep breath that tasted of smoke and moonlight and possibility, he began to drop them one by one into the waiting cups.

The first stone fell into its cup with a sound that echoed in spaces beyond the physical—a note struck on an instrument tuned to frequencies only the soul could hear. Micah continued dropping stones counterclockwise, one in each cup, the ancient rhythm of the game asserting itself. Such a simple action, yet his hand trembled slightly, knowing that each placement was being read, interpreted, judged.

His fourth stone landed in a cup on Eldrazi's side, and by the game's rules, he captured it along with the stones in the opposite cup. His first successful move. Seven stones gathered to his side, added to his store. A small victory that felt larger in the silver moonlight.

"Aggressive," Eldrazi noted, her voice neutral as still water. "Beginning with capture rather than building. Your great-grandfather Harold would be proud. He believed in taking what could be taken, quickly, before opportunity passed."

She reached for her own cups, selecting the fourth from her right. Her movements were fluid, practiced, the stones flowing from cup to cup like water finding its course. She played three moves to his one, setting up patterns he couldn't yet see, creating possibilities that would bloom in future rounds.

"But aggression without foundation is merely hunger," she continued as her final stone landed, capturing nothing but repositioning everything. "The game rewards patience as much as boldness. Understanding as much as action."

Micah studied the changed board. Already the simple beginning position had transformed into something complex, stones clustered unevenly, some cups empty and waiting, others heavy with possibility. He could see three moves ahead, maybe four, but beyond that the patterns multiplied into chaos.

He selected his third cup, began distributing its stones. As they fell, memories not his own flickered at the edges of consciousness—other men's hands on these same stones, young and trembling. Other families, other attempts, other failures layering like sediment in his awareness.

"Does the board remember?" he asked as his turn ended. "All the games played before?"

"Everything remembers," Eldrazi replied, considering her next move. "Stones remember the mountains they came from. Wood remembers its tree. Games remember their players. Yes, the board knows every hand that has touched it, every pattern that has been played across its surface."

She moved, a long cascade of stones that seemed to re-structure the entire board. Cups that had been full emptied, empty ones filled, the whole pattern shifting like a living thing. When she finished, she had captured twelve of his stones in a single sequence.

"But you are also playing with their learning," she added, gathering the captured stones to her side. "Each failure teaches. Each loss adds to the board's wisdom. Perhaps that knowledge bleeds through, if a player is quiet enough to hear it."

The silver sand in the hourglass rose steadily, defying earthly physics with serene certainty. Perhaps a quarter had passed—or was it less? Time moved strangely here, each moment stretching or compressing according to its own logic.

Micah forced himself to breathe slowly, to think. Eldrazi was clearly the superior player in terms of pure strategy. Centuries of practice against desperate opponents had honed her skills to perfection. But she'd said winning wasn't about skill alone. The game read hearts, not just minds.

What did his heart want? Freedom, yes. Life unburdened by ancestral weight. But deeper than that, what?

He thought of David, protected by faith Micah had been too proud to accept. Thought of all the invitations refused, all the hands extended and not taken. He'd walked into this forest partly from despair, partly from having nowhere else to go. But also from something else—a deep, wordless need to face whatever his ancestors had fled from. To stop running, even if stopping meant destruction.

His next move came from that place. Instead of aggressive like his first, it was something else. Tactical. He selected a cup that would gain him no captures, no immediate advantage. But it would create a pattern—stones arranged in a Fibonacci sequence across three cups. Mathematics made manifest. Beauty for its own sake.

Eldrazi's eyes sharpened. "Interesting."

"My mother loved patterns," Micah said, watching her consider her response. "She'd do genealogy for hours, not just collecting names but finding the rhythms in family lines. She saw our curse before anyone else, just by mapping the numbers. Death before 40. Always young, always tragic, but also always patterned. I think maybe she was worried for me. She was trying to nail down when my time would be up."

"And you inherit her eye." Eldrazi moved, but carefully now, respecting the pattern he'd created even as she worked to dismantle it.

They traded moves in silence for a while, the only sounds the click of stones and crack of burning wood. The game developed complexity, patterns emerging and dissolving like frost on glass. Sometimes Eldrazi dominated, capturing stones in sweeping moves that spoke of long experience. Sometimes Micah found sequences she hadn't expected, small victories that earned what might have been approval in her ancient eyes.

"Tell me about the forest," Micah said as he contemplated a difficult position. "How does a place like this come to be? How does it call to specific bloodlines?"

"Places of power exist where they need to exist," Eldrazi answered, making a move that opened three different paths for attack. "When Rebecca fled west, her pain and power sought a home. The curse she spoke needed a crucible, a place to play out. The forest was already old, already touched by older magic than hers. It accepted her offering, became the stage where her words would find their truth or falsehood."

"So it's conscious? Alive?"

"As conscious as a river that knows how to find the sea. As alive as winter that knows when to become spring." She captured more stones, adding to her growing hoard. "It has purpose rather than thought, will rather than desire. It shows the truth in all its terrible glory. No malice in it, no kindness. Only purpose."

Micah made his move, saw immediately it was a mistake. Eldrazi could capture nearly half his remaining stones if she saw the opening. But instead of pouncing, she paused, studying not the board but him.

"You're tired," she observed.

He was. The tremor was back in his hands, and his vision kept trying to blur. Days without real food, nights without real sleep, trials that had burned through what little reserves he'd had. His body was failing in real time, systems shutting down in the careful sequence of starvation.

"I can continue," he said.

"I know you can. The question is whether you should." She made her move—not the devastating capture he'd left open, but a quieter play that extended the game. "Pride and determination are not the same thing. Stubbornness and strength are not the same thing. The board knows the difference."

"Are you offering me mercy?"

"I am offering you nothing. The game offers what it offers." She gestured to the hourglass, where silver sand continued its impossible ascent. "Time remains. Moves remain. You remain, for now. Play or do not play, but choose from wisdom rather than pride."

"Show me the rest," he said, reaching for his stones.

Eldrazi smiled—not kindly, but with something like respect. "Very well. But remember—each vision shows not just their failure but their opportunity. The invitation was always there. The question is whether you'll accept it when your moment comes."

Micah selected his next move carefully, knowing that with each stone placed, each vision endured, he moved closer to his own moment of truth. The game continued under the watching moon, and somewhere in the darkness beyond the firelight, the forest held its breath.

Micah lifted the stones from the fifth cup, and again the world dissolved.

This time he was Harold Thorne, standing in a church basement. His hands—Harold's hands—were rough from factory work, stained with the grease that never quite washed clean. Through Harold's eyes, Micah saw the room: folding chairs arranged in rows, a table with coffee and store-bought cookies, a hand-painted banner reading "Building Fund - Together in Faith."

The lockbox sat open on the table. Three thousand dollars in cash and checks—more money than Harold had ever seen in one place. His stomach clenched with a hunger that wasn't Micah's. Margaret hadn't eaten meat in two weeks. The children—Micah's grandfather among them—were wearing shoes held together with tape.

Through Harold's memory, Micah felt the bone-deep exhaustion of working double shifts only to watch the bills multiply faster than the paychecks. The weight of being a provider who couldn't provide. The shame that curdled into rage, then despair, then something harder and more danger-ous: the conviction that the world owed him more than this.

Pastor Clark's voice echoed from the sanctuary above. "Harold Thorne has accepted our invitation to serve as trea-surer. A man who understands struggle, who can guide others through hardship with faith intact."

The invitation had come that morning, unexpected as grace. *You're a good man, Harold. The congregation needs lead-ers who understand what it means to go without, to struggle and still believe. Men who can show others that faith isn't about prosperity but presence.*

Harold stared at the money. Three thousand dollars. Enough to catch up on rent, buy shoes that fit, put meat on the table. Enough to stop the looks Margaret gave him when she thought he wasn't watching. It wasn't even accusation. Somehow that would have been better. Worse, her expression held understanding. Understanding that he was drowning and she couldn't save him.

The treasurer position meant visibility. Accountability. Sunday mornings standing before the congregation, speak-ing about God when Harold hadn't prayed since he could remember. It meant Wednesday night Bible studies and visiting the sick and counseling other men who'd lost their way—when Harold could barely find his own path.

It meant choosing to be more than his circumstances. Choosing faith over flight.

Too hard, Harold thought. *Too much to ask of a man already carrying more than he could bear.*

The money whispered easier promises. Take it. Blame the colored janitor—nobody would question that. Or say nothing, let them think someone broke in. Either way, catch the evening train west. California had jobs, sunshine, anonymity. California didn't know Harold Thorne was drowning.

Through Harold's memories, Micah saw the moment stretch like taffy. The same crossroads Ezekiel had faced, dressed in different clothes. Choose the difficult right or the easy wrong. Accept the calling that would demand everything or take the escape that promised comfort.

Harold's hand moved toward the money. Paused.

Pastor Clark's voice drifted down: "Leadership isn't about being perfect. It's about being present. About showing up even when—especially when—it's hard."

Harold's hand closed on the bills. The choice made in an instant, playing out the same pattern that had befallen previous generations. He stuffed the money into his coat, closed the lockbox, and walked up the stairs. Passed Pastor Clark without meeting his eyes. Out into the Charlestown evening where the train station waited.

But Micah was still in Harold's mind as the scene shifted. California, years later. Harold dying badly in a factory accident that shouldn't have been fatal—crushed by machinery he was too tired to operate safely because he worked three jobs to maintain the illusion of success. In those final moments, clarity:

He'd run from the treasurer position, but leadership had found him anyway. Foreman, union rep, positions that demanded what he'd never developed: integrity under pressure. Each time, when the weight grew heavy, Harold chose the familiar pattern. Shortcuts. Lies. Eventually theft again, though he called it "borrowing from the pension fund."

The invitation had been real. Not just to church leadership but to learn how to carry weight without breaking. To develop spiritual strength through daily practice. To become the man his family needed by submitting to something greater than his own broken judgment.

Instead, he'd chosen the pattern. Easy money over hard growth. Flight over faith. And taught his sons—Micah's grandfather among them—that when life gets heavy, you run. When God calls, you hide. When the hard path appears, you take the easy one, no matter who pays the price.

The vision shattered. Micah gasped back into his own body, tears streaming down his face. Not for Harold's theft but for his loss. The life he could have lived. The man he could have become. The protection he could have offered his children through example instead of absence.

"He was so tired," Micah whispered. "So beaten down. The money must have seemed like—"

"Like salvation," Eldrazi finished. "Yes. The easy path always does. That's its power. In the moment of choosing, comfort whispers louder than conscience. The immediate relief drowns out the distant consequences."

She moved her stones, taking two more of his. "But notice what the invitation offered. Not wealth. Not ease. But a structure for becoming stronger. Daily accountability. Weekly practice at speaking truth. Regular opportunities to serve others despite his own struggles. The very things that would have prepared him for the weight life kept placing on his shoulders."

"David's family has that," Micah said slowly. "The structure. The practice. The... muscle memory of choosing right even when it's hard."

"Built over generations. Each father teaching his son not through words but through example. How to show up when you'd rather hide. How to give when you'd rather hoard. How to trust when you'd rather control. Small choices, daily made, building strength for when the large choices come."

Micah stared at the board. His position was weakening with each exchange, but he began to understand this wasn't really about winning or losing. It was about seeing. Understanding. Recognizing the pattern so he could choose differently when—

When.

Not if.

His moment would come. Was coming. Perhaps had already begun the moment he'd entered the forest instead of taking whatever pills remained in his medicine cabinet. The game would show him what he needed to see, and then...

Then he would face his own crossroads. And unlike Eze-kiel, unlike Harold, unlike all who came before, he would have seen the full weight of what choosing the easy path truly cost.

"Your move," Eldrazi said softly. "One more vision awaits. One more truth the game must show. Are you ready to see how close to home the pattern comes?"

Micah reached for the stones, knowing the next vision would hit hardest. Knowing it would show him his own reflection in the mirror of generational failure. Knowing it would strip away any last illusion that he was different, better, somehow exempt from the pattern he'd been born into.

His hand closed on the smooth obsidian. The forest watched. The moon waited.

The stones fell, and Micah tumbled into memory. Not ancient history, but a sharp-edged recollection from less than a year ago. Thanksgiving at Aunt Carol's house, the noise of family gathering pressing against his skull like a vice.

He was himself but also outside himself, watching his own choices with the clarity the game forced upon all who played it. Through the kitchen window, he could see the version of himself from last November, escaping to the back porch with a beer that would be followed by three more before dinner.

David found him there, because David always found him. That was his cousin's gift—or curse—the inability to let people disappear even when they wanted to.

"Hey man." David settled onto the porch steps, produc-ing two bottles from behind his back. Good beer, not the cheap stuff Micah had grabbed. "Figured you might want company."

Through the strange double vision of memory and observation, Micah watched himself take the beer, watched the way his past self's shoulders stayed rigid, defensive. Ready to deflect whatever well-meaning assault on his solitude was coming.

"You doing okay?" David asked, and the genuine concern in his voice was harder to defend against than judgment would have been. "I know holidays are rough. First Thanksgiving since Sarah..."

"I'm fine." The lie came so easily. Had always come easily. Fine was the password that kept people from looking too close, from seeing the carefully maintained emptiness where a person should be.

David took a sip of his beer, let the silence stretch. Inside, Aunt Carol's laughter rang bright as church bells. Someone had started the football game. Normal sounds of a normal family gathering that felt like they were coming from another planet.

"Look," David said finally, "I wanted to run something by you. No pressure. But there's this group at church—young adults, mostly. We meet Thursday nights. Nothing heavy, just... hanging out. Talking about life. Sometimes we talk about God, sometimes we just play board games badly and eat too much pizza."

Micah felt it again—that moment of possibility. Through the game's vision, he could see what his past self couldn't: the lifeline being thrown. This was not an invitation to a social group but to a *practice*. A weekly commitment to showing up. To being seen. To letting others carry some of the weight he'd been shouldering alone since his parents died.

But his past self heard only the word "church" and everything it implied. Judgment. Expectations. Having to pretend at faith he didn't feel. Having to be around people who had their lives together while his was systematically falling apart.

"Maybe later," past-Micah said. "I'm pretty busy right now."

The lie tasted like ash. Like Ezekiel's lie. Like Harold's rationalization. The same words in different mouths across generations: *Later. When I'm ready. When I have more time. When I'm better.*

David's face—God, Micah had forgotten that expression. Understanding. Not disappointment but understanding. Just like Harold had seen on his wife's face. Were they all so transparent, so naked to world in their weakness?

"The offer stands," David said simply. "Always. And Micah? You don't have to believe anything. Don't have to have answers. Hell, half the group is just trying to figure out what questions to ask. But you do have to show up. That's the only requirement. Just... show up."

Through the vision, Micah could see what followed that refusal. The weeks sliding into months. The depression deepening like water finding its level. The phone calls ignored, the invitations declined, the systematic severing of every connection that might have held him to life.

He watched himself choose isolation because isolation was controllable. Choose cynicism because cynicism was safe. Choose the familiar despair over the terrifying possibility of hope.

But the game showed him more—what he'd missed by refusing. Not just pizza and board games but practice. David's group wrestling with doubt together instead of alone. Learning to voice fears without shame. Building the muscle memory of vulnerability, of showing up even when—especially when—they'd rather hide.

One Thursday became another became another. Habits forming. Friendships deepening. Faith not as certainty but as choice, daily made, to keep walking even when the path was unclear. The same structure that had saved David's father and grandfather. Just the simple discipline of choosing connection over isolation, community over control, the hard work of being known over the easy anonymity of hiding.

"What if they judge me?" past-Micah had thought but not said.

"What if they don't?" present-Micah whispered to a memory that couldn't hear him.

The vision shifted, showing what came after. The accelerating spiral. The job lost because showing up became impossible. Sarah leaving with no malice, but with the exhausted sorrow of someone who'd tried to love a ghost. The nights staring at the ceiling, counting water stains, feeling the weight of his bloodline pressing down like dirt on a coffin.

And through it all, David's offer echoing: *Just show up.*

Such a small thing. Such an impossible thing. The first step onto the hard path his ancestors had all refused. Not "find faith" or "get better" or "figure it all out." Just show up. Let yourself be seen. Trust that broken people gathering together might become something more than the sum of their damage.

Micah had chosen the pattern instead. The comfortable isolation. The manageable despair. The known quantity of slowly dying over the unknown risk of trying to live.

The vision released him, and he found himself back at the game board, tears streaming down his face. Not for his ancestors now but for himself. For the life he'd been offered and refused. For the protection he could have had—not from suffering but from suffering alone.

"I was no different," he said. "I made the same choice."

"Yes," Eldrazi said gently. "But you also made a different choice. You're here. In my forest. Playing this game. That, too, matters."

"Does it?" The bitterness in his voice surprised him. "Or am I just choosing a different kind of running? Trading slow suicide for a dramatic exit?"

The old woman studied him with eyes that had seen too much to be surprised by human frailty. "Perhaps. Many who find my forest seek only an ending with more meaning than pills or bridges. But you followed the fox. Endured the trials. Came to play the game. These are not the actions of someone seeking only escape."

"Then what am I seeking?"

"The same thing every Thorne man has sought when the weight becomes unbearable. A way back. The difference is you're willing to see what that way demands. Your ancestors saw and turned aside. You see and continue."

She gestured to the board where his position had grown desperate. Few stones remained to him, while hers were plentiful. "One more move each, and then we see if you're ready for the choice the game has been preparing you to make. Win or lose, live or die—these are small things compared to who you choose to be in the choosing."

Micah looked at his remaining stones, understanding now that the game had never been about victory. It had been about vision. About seeing clearly the pattern that had trapped his bloodline, the invitations they'd refused, the price of always choosing the easy path.

Now, armed with that sight, he would face his own crossroads.

He selected his stones for what might be his final move, ready to see what truth the game would reveal when the playing was done.

Micah placed his stones with deliberate care, watching them fall into cups that seemed to deepen with each piece dropped. The sound echoed longer than it should have, rippling outward into the forest like rings in dark water.

For a moment, nothing happened. Then the fire flared between them, casting new shadows, and in those shadows Micah saw himself.

It wasn't memory he saw this time, but something that may yet be. Two paths diverging from this moment, each as real as the other, waiting for him to choose which future would take flesh.

In the first vision, he saw himself losing the game. Not through poor play but through the same choice his ancestors had made—stopping before the end, walking away and choosing ease instead of risk. He watched himself return to the world, lying to himself that his newfound understanding would be enough, that he didn't need the transformation. Knowing why his family suffered but choosing the familiar suffering over the unknown demands of breaking free.

That Micah lived carefully. Avoided connections that might demand vulnerability. Worked jobs that required nothing deeper than showing up. Died the day before his fortieth—later than his father but earlier than he might have—of what the coroner would call heart failure but what was really the accumulated weight of a life half-lived. The pattern continued, diluted perhaps but unbroken. Any son he might have would inherit the same tendency toward isolation, the same fear of the hard path, the same curse dressed in different clothes.

In the second vision, he saw something else.

He saw himself finishing the game—win or lose didn't matter, only that he played to the end. Saw himself choosing to risk everything on the possibility of transformation. If he won, the curse would break, yes. But if he lost...

If he lost, he would remain in the forest. Not dead, exactly, but not alive in any way the world would recognize. Another spirit among the trees, a whisper in the fog, a warning or guide for the next seeker who came looking for answers. His body would join the memorial clearing, his belongings neatly arranged with the others who'd chosen transformation over return.

But even in losing, he would have chosen differently than his fathers. Would have played to the end instead of fleeing at the crucial moment. That choice—to see it through, to accept the consequences, to stop running—would echo forward too.

"Do you see?" Eldrazi asked softly. "The game itself is the trial. Not winning or losing but choosing to play fully, knowing the cost. Your ancestors saw what change would demand and chose the certainty of curse over the uncertainty of transformation. What do you choose?"

Micah stared at the board. His position was nearly hopeless—three stones to her dozen. One more exchange and the game would end. He could walk away now, as his fathers had. Take his understanding back to the world and use it to live more carefully, if not more fully. It would be enough. More than his ancestors had managed. A small victory.

Or he could play the final moves and accept whatever came.

The fox stirred from its place by the fire, padding over to sit beside him. Its warmth pressed against his leg—the first time in obvious, palpable affection since entering the forest. In that touch, a message: *Whatever you choose, you won't be alone in the choosing.*

"There's something else," Micah said slowly. "Something you haven't told me."

Eldrazi smiled—the first genuine warmth he'd seen from her. "Clever boy. Yes. The game has one more secret. Win or lose, those who play to the end earn a gift."

"What gift?"

"The chance to begin again. Not as you were but as you might be. The forest keeps those who lose, yes, but not in death. In service. Guides for the lost. Guardians of the threshold. Witnesses to the possibility of choice." She gestured to the fox beside him. "Some served so long and well they earned new forms, new purposes. But all chose their fate with full knowledge. That, too, is a kind of victory."

Micah understood then. His ancestors hadn't just fled from losing—they'd fled from winning. Because whether he broke the curse or became part of the forest's mystery, he would be transformed. Changed beyond recognition. The comfortable misery of his old life would be impossible to return to.

"And if I win?" he asked. "If I break the curse?"

She leaned forward, firelight dancing in her ancient eyes. "The curse breaks, yes. But curses are easy compared to blessings. Blessings must be chosen, again and again, every day until the choosing becomes nature. That's the real reason your ancestors walked away. Not fear of losing but fear of what winning would require."

Micah looked at his three remaining stones. Such small things to hold such weight. But that was the lesson, wasn't it? Every choice seemed small in the moment. Lying about a neighbor for personal gain. Stealing from the church. Refusing David's invitation. Small stones dropped into cups, creating patterns that echoed through generations.

He thought of David, showing up every Thursday night. Not because he had answers but because he'd learned that sometimes the showing up was the answer. Building strength through repetition. Faith through practice. Community through the simple act of being present.

"I'll finish the game," Micah said.

The words hung in the air like a vow. The fire crackled. The moon watched. Even the forest seemed to lean in, ancient trees bearing witness to this moment they'd seen before but never quite like this.

"Then make your final move," Eldrazi said formally. "And let us see which future takes flesh tonight."

Micah gathered his last three stones. His hand was steady now, the trembling that had plagued him since entering the forest finally stilled. Not through health returned but through certainty found. Whatever came next—victory or defeat, transformation or transcendence—he would meet it with eyes open.

He began to place his stones, ready to discover what lay beyond the pattern that had defined his bloodline for so long. The game would end tonight. But something else—something his forefathers had been too frightened to name—would begin.

CHAPTER 8:
THE WEIGHT OF FATHERS

Micah's store held twelve stones now. Eldrazi's held eighteen. The math was unkind but not impossible. The moon had moved—or seemed to have moved—hours passing in what felt like minutes, or minutes stretching into eternities. Time had stopped meaning anything except the rhythm of stones dropping into cups.

His hands ached from gripping the smooth obsidian pieces. His back protested the hours spent hunched over the board. Real physical discomforts that anchored him to his body even as the visions threatened to dissolve the boundaries of self entirely. The fire had burned low, the long shadows made Eldrazi's face shift between ancient and ageless with each flicker.

"Your game is improving," Eldrazi observed, making her next move with practiced ease. Three stones clicked into place with a sound like distant thunder. "You've learned from watching your fathers' failures. But learning isn't the same as choosing. Soon you'll face your own moment. We'll see then if you're truly different."

The words settled into Micah's chest like stones in deep water. He studied the board, seeing patterns within patterns—not just the game itself but the larger design it represented. Each cup a generation, each stone a choice, the whole thing a map of inherited failure stretching back to Salem's bitter soil.

His hand hovered over the next cup. He knew what was coming—another vision, another ancestor, another moment where the hard path was rejected for the easy one. His father was next. Had to be. The game demanded it.

Michael Thorne. Dead at thirty-nine on a rain-slick highway, taking Micah's mother with him. Two years ago now, though it felt both like yesterday and a lifetime past. Micah had spent those years constructing his father from fragments—the smell of sawdust and beer, rough hands teaching him to tie fishing flies, a laugh that came easy after the third drink but never quite reached his eyes.

He almost didn't want to see. Didn't want to watch his father fail, to experience that failure from the inside. The other visions had been hard enough—strangers connected by blood but not memory. This would be different. This would hurt in ways the others hadn't.

But the game wouldn't let him refuse. The only way out was through.

The fox shifted in the shadows beyond the firelight, a subtle movement that drew Micah's attention. Those amber eyes held something like encouragement, or perhaps just witness. No longer his guide through physical forests but through the darker woods of family history.

"Your hesitation speaks well of you," Eldrazi said, her voice softer than before. "So many others reached for the stones eagerly, thinking each vision brought them closer to winning. They didn't understand that every revelation was also a weight to carry. That knowing the truth doesn't make it lighter."

Micah thought of Harold stealing from the collection plate, young and desperate and so sure God wouldn't notice. Of Ezekiel choosing land over truth, betraying a neighbor for gain but winning nothing but a curse. Of his own moment with David—*Come to church with me, Micah. You don't have to believe*—and how he'd chosen isolation over the possibility of grace.

He understood their logic, their fear, their terrible certainty that the easy choice was the only choice. That was the real curse—the accumulated stain of small surrenders, each generation teaching the next that hardship was to be avoided, that comfort mattered more than character.

His stomach twisted with hunger. How long had they been playing? The forest beyond their circle of firelight gave no clues—it could have been hours or days. His water was gone, his throat dry despite the stream somewhere in the darkness. But these discomforts felt distant compared to the ache of what was coming.

"I need to see," he said finally, surprised by the steadiness of his own voice. "I need to know who he really was."

He'd always known the mental fragments he held of his father were edited. The good memories polished smooth by grief, the bad ones sharpened by adolescent resentment. The real man, faced with choices that mattered, revealing himself through what he chose when it cost something to choose.

Micah picked up the stones. Six of them, smooth and heavy, holding heat from his palm. He counted them twice—an old habit from childhood, when precision felt like protection against chaos. Then he let them fall, his hand moving counterclockwise around the board, dropping a single stone with soft clicks that echoed in the clearing. First stone, second stone, third. . The last stone circled the rim of its cup before dropping, and with it, Micah fell too—

Into summer heat and the smell of pine sap, into a body twenty-two years young and strong with untested strength, into a moment forty years past when Michael Thorne faced a choice that would echo through time.

Micah was his father, hiking a trail he'd walked a dozen times before. The familiar disorientation of becoming some-one else—different height, different gait, different weight to his steps—lasted only moments before Michael's memories flooded in. Weekend warrior, his friends called him. Every Saturday morning found him on these trails, escaping the suffocation of his job and the apartment that smelled like his roommate's weed.

The pack on his shoulders held lunch, water, a first aid kit his mother had insisted on. She worried too much, but he car-ried it anyway. The trail wound upward through second-growth redwoods, not the ancient giants deeper in the park but still impressive enough to make him feel small and insignificant.

He'd been hiking for two hours, making good time. The summit vista was another hour ahead—his favorite spot where the forest opened to show the Pacific stretching endless and blue. He'd eat his sandwich there, maybe read for a while, definitely some photos. Simple plans for a simple day.

Then he rounded the bend and saw it.

The redwood had fallen recently, probably in last week's storm. Its trunk stretched across the trail like a barricade, wider than a car, bark still damp with morning fog. The root ball towered above him on one side, a wall of earth and twisted wood. The crown disappeared into the ravine on the other, taking out smaller trees in its fall.

Michael stopped, considering. The tree completely blocked the path. He could see where other hikers had scrambled around—a steep, sketchy traverse across loose soil and poison oak. Doable, but not pleasant. His legs were long enough to make it work.

That's when he heard the voices.

From the other side of the massive trunk came sounds of distress—a man's frustrated muttering, a woman's soothing tones, and underneath it all, a child crying. They came into view slowly, working their way around the crown end of the tree where the branches made passage nearly impossible.

The man appeared first, carrying a toddler who couldn't have been more than two. Red-faced from exertion, sweat staining his t-shirt despite the morning cool. Behind him, a woman held the hand of a four-year-old girl who was trying very hard not to cry like her little sister.

"Thank God," the man said when he saw Michael. "Is there a way through on that side?"

Michael looked at the steep scramble, then at the family. The father's hiking boots were decent but the mother wore tennis shoes. The kids had those tiny sneakers that were more decoration than function. No way they'd make it across that traverse safely.

"It's pretty sketchy," Michael admitted. "Steep and loose. How far have you come?"

"Two miles from the parking area," the woman said. She looked tired already, a day pack sagging on her shoulders. "We promised Emma we'd see the waterfall. It's her birthday."

The waterfall. Another mile past where the tree had fallen. Michael's heart sank a little. His peaceful summit lunch was evaporating before his eyes.

He looked at the tree again, really looked at it. The trunk was massive but not impossible. If they could shift it even a few feet, create a gap near the root end where the diameter was smaller, maybe stack some rocks to make steps over the lower portion... It would work. Two men could do it, especially with the woman helping where she could. Hard work, maybe an hour of effort. His back would complain—he'd tweaked it at work lifting boxes last week. But it was possible.

The right thing to do was obvious. Help them move the tree. Make the trail passable not just for this family but for everyone who'd come after. That's what community meant, wasn't it? That's what his father would have done, back before the drinking got bad. That's what decent people did.

But...

His summit. His one day off this week. The photo he'd keep forever and post on his wall for all to see. His back really did hurt. And he'd been looking forward to this all week, counting down the hours until he could be alone in the woods, no customers, no manager, no roommate's music through thin walls.

And really, wasn't it the park service's job to clear trails? He didn't see a uniform on his back. Wasn't getting paid for manual labor. Had done his share of that this week already.

The inner voice came quiet but insistent: *Help them. This is why you're here. Not for photos but for this moment, this choice. Serve. Choose hard.*

Louder voice, more reasonable: *Too much. Too hard. Not your problem. The rangers will clear it eventually. Or someone else will. Someone with better tools, more time, a stronger back.*

Michael found himself speaking before he'd consciously decided. "There's a way around on this side. Pretty steep but doable if you're careful. I can help you across."

It wasn't a lie, technically. He could help them navigate the traverse, make sure they didn't slip. That was helping, wasn't it? That counted.

"We can't," the father said immediately. "Not with the kids. Emma already took one fall today—that's enough adventure. Is there another trail to the waterfall?"

"Not from this side," Michael said, hating himself a little for the relief he felt. "You'd have to go back to the parking area, drive twenty minutes to the north entrance. Probably not worth it with little ones."

He watched the family's faces fall. The birthday girl— Emma—finally let those tears come. The father's jaw tightened with the particular frustration of promises broken by circumstances. The mother knelt beside her daughter, murmuring comfort.

"It's okay, sweetie. We'll come back another day when the trail's fixed. We can still have a picnic by the parking area. Remember that meadow with all the flowers?"

Michael felt the moment crystallizing around him, heavy with significance he couldn't quite name. The tree lay between them like a test. Not from God—he didn't believe in that anymore—but from something. The universe, maybe. Basic human decency.

He could suggest they work together to move it. Could offer his back and his strength and his time. Could turn this disappointed birthday into something memorable—the day strangers worked together, the day Emma helped clear a trail, the day obstruction became opportunity.

"Well," he said instead, "good luck. Happy birthday, Emma."

He turned away before their faces could guilt him into reconsidering. The traverse was indeed sketchy, requiring handholds on exposed roots and careful foot placement above the drop. His long legs made it manageable. Behind him, he heard the family's voices grow fainter as they began their disappointed trek back.

The rest of his hike felt hollow. The summit vista spread before him exactly as beautiful as always, but the sandwich tasted like cardboard and the photos felt performative. He kept thinking about the tree, about the hour of work that would have cleared it. About Emma's tears and her father's frustration and her mother's gentle acceptance of one more small disappointment.

On the way down, the tree was still there. Of course it was. No trail fairy had magically moved it. The traverse looked even worse in the afternoon light, shadows hiding the good footholds. He made it across again, but barely, one foot slipping enough to spike his heart rate.

The parking lot was empty when he reached it. The family long gone to their Plan B picnic. He sat in his car for a long moment, key in the ignition, feeling like he'd failed something important.

Two weeks later, a sixty-five-year-old hiker named Margaret Chen would try to navigate that same traverse. She'd slip on the loose soil, fall twenty feet into the ravine, and break her hip. Search and rescue would take six hours to reach her. She'd survive but never hike again.

Michael would never know this. Would never connect his choice to its consequences. That was how the curse worked. But sitting in his car that day, he felt it settling into his bones. Another Thorne man walking away from the hard right thing. Another link in a chain stretching back to Salem and forward to a son not yet born who would inherit both his father's eyes and his tendency to choose the easy path—

Micah gasped back into his own body, his father's choice sitting heavy as the fallen tree in his chest. His hands shook as he set down the remaining stones. Such a small thing. Such an easy thing to rationalize. But it revealed everything—the pattern of avoidance, the refusal to do hard things even when they were right, the choice of self over service that defined every man in his line.

"I could see it," he whispered to Eldrazi. "Could see exactly what he should have done. Why didn't he?"

"Why didn't you go to church with David?" she asked gently. "Why didn't Ezekiel tell the truth? The answer is always the same—because choosing right is harder than choosing easy."

The fox padded into the firelight, settling beside Eldrazi, eyes fixed on Micah with an expression almost like compassion.

"But David—" Micah began.

"David moves the tree," Eldrazi finished. "Every time. Even when his back hurts. Even when he has plans. Even when it's not his job. That's the difference. That's why the curse can't touch him."

Micah thought of his cousin—steady, reliable David who showed up early to help with church events he didn't organize, who visited elderly neighbors he didn't know well, who did the small invisible kindnesses that nobody thanked him for. Not because he was naturally better but because he chose to be, one decision at a time.

"My father wasn't a bad man," Micah said, needing it to be true.

"No," Eldrazi agreed. "Just a man who chose easy over hard, over and over, until choosing easy was all he knew how to do. The tree was still there when he died, Micah. Almost twenty years later. Nobody ever moved it. The trail closed eventually. The waterfall path forgotten. All to avoid an hour's work on a Saturday morning."

The game board waited between them, patient as time. Micah's next move would complete the round, trigger the complex counting that might swing the game in his favor. Or might not. The stones didn't care about his realizations, his grief, his growing understanding. They followed older rules than human emotion.

The silence stretched between them, broken only by the fire's quiet conversation with itself. Micah stared at the board, seeing his father's face in the polished obsidian, seeing every moment Michael Thorne had chosen the easy path. Not a monster. Just a man who'd perfected the art of walking around obstacles instead of through them.

The fox made a sound that might have been agreement, a soft chirp that seemed to come from somewhere deeper than its throat. Its eyes reflected the firelight like amber mirrors, showing Micah his own face transformed by shadow and flame.

Micah thought of his own life with new clarity. Every hard conversation avoided because confrontation made his stomach hurt. Every relationship he'd let die rather than fight for because fighting meant vulnerability. Every opportunity declined because it required effort, risk, the possibility of failure. Every time he'd chosen isolation over connection, cynicism over hope, giving up over pushing through.

"I'm just like them," he whispered. The words tasted like ashes.

She moved again, a complex play that seemed to shift the entire dynamic of the board. Micah saw his position weakening, opportunities closing, the path to victory narrowing to a thread. "Fear overrode belief. Time again, fear won out."

"But they all believed. Well, most of them. Everyone did back then."

"Faith isn't belief," she continued. "Of course your ancestors believed. They all believed in God, in heaven, in hell. There was no other option. No allowable way to even voice a doubt. Belief is easy—it lives in the head, costs nothing, demands nothing. Faith is choosing. Faith is doing."

"And they rejected faith," Micah said, thinking of his father's bitter comments about church, stories of his grandfather's whiskey-soaked dismissals of religion, the long line of Thorne men who'd walked away from God. "They became atheists, agnostics, critics."

"They rejected the *demands* of faith," Eldrazi corrected. "Easier to say God doesn't exist than to admit He does and you're failing Him. Easier to mock believers than to join them in the hard work of service. Your father didn't stop believing because of some intellectual argument. He stopped because faith wanted him to move trees, and moving trees is hard."

The truth of it hit Micah like cold water. Every philosophical objection his father had raised, every clever argument against religion—they'd all been elaborate ways of saying *too hard*. The universe is meaningless? Easier than a universe where choices matter. Morality is relative? Easier than absolute standards you're failing to meet. Prayer is talking to yourself? Easier than talking to Someone who might answer with uncomfortable truths.

"David never argues theology," Micah said slowly. "Never tries to convince anyone. He just... shows up."

"And the curse can't touch him." Eldrazi's smile was sad and ancient. "Not because he's special. Not because God plays favorites. Curses feed on the space between what we should do and what we choose to do. David keeps that space small. Your family let it grow into a chasm."

The fox stretched in his position by Micah's leg, its fur bristling long its back. . It seemed to Micah a gesture to remind him of its presence.

"What about my mother?" Micah asked suddenly. "She died with my father. Was she cursed too?"

"Your mother chose your father," Eldrazi said gently. "Loved him despite his flaws. Tried to fill the spaces he left empty. But one person can't carry faith for two. She moved her trees, but she couldn't make him move his. In the end, his choices killed them both."

The unfairness of it burned in Micah's chest. His mother paying for his father's pattern, dying because Michael Thorne was too stubborn to get the car serviced, too proud to admit the brakes felt soft, too committed to easy to spend money on maintenance.

"That's why the curse passes to sons," he realized. "Because we learn from our fathers. Learn to walk around instead of through. Learn that caring costs too much, that helping hurts too much, that faith asks too much."

"But you can unlearn." Eldrazi gestured to the board. "That's why we play. So you can see the power was always within your grasp."

Micah made his move, stones falling into cups with quiet finality.

"When my moment comes," he said, "how will I know?"

Eldrazi's laughter was like wind through old trees. "Oh, child. You'll know. The hard choice always announces itself. It's the one that makes your stomach clench, your pride rebel, your fear scream. It's the tree in the path that would be so easy to walk around. So reasonable to leave for someone else. So justifiable to ignore."

"What if I'm too weak, too much my father's son?"

"Then you'll die young like all the Thorne men before you. And your son—if you ever have one—will sit where you sit, holding the same stones, facing the same choice, carrying the same curse… if he makes it this far." She leaned forward, firelight dancing across her ancient face. "But you've seen what they couldn't see. Known what they refused to know. The pattern is clear now, the momentum understood. The only question is whether understanding is enough to overcome inheritance."

The game had shifted while they talked, subtle alignments clicking into place like tumblers in a lock. Micah counted stones again—fifteen in his store now, twenty-one in hers. But the board itself told a different story. Three of his cups positioned perfectly for a sweeping play, if he could just navigate the next two moves correctly. He was not yet winning, but no longer losing.

The possibility of victory made his hands shake.

"Your move," Eldrazi said simply. No encouragement, no warning. Just fact.

Micah studied the board with new eyes. Each cup connected to others in patterns he was only beginning to understand—not just the game's rules but the deeper design they reflected. Choices leading to choices, consequences spreading like ripples, the whole thing a map of cause and effect that stretched from Salem to this impossible moment.

The fox had moved again, craning its neck to look up at him. Waiting. Watching. Witnessing what came next.

He reached for the stones in the third cup—the obvious move, the safe play that would protect his position without risking much. His fingers closed around them, and the vision hit like thunder.

He saw himself at this same board, minutes or hours from now. The game balanced on a knife's edge, victory and defeat separated by a single stone's placement. Eldrazi waiting with infinite patience. The fox alert with anticipation. And in his hands, a choice that would echo through generations.

The easy play: defensive, careful, protecting what he'd gained. It would probably lose him the game eventually, but slowly, safely. No risk. No cost. The kind of move his father would make, had made, every time life offered a chance to reach for more.

The hard play: aggressive, sacrificial, exposing himself to loss in pursuit of something greater. It would either win everything or lose everything. No middle ground. No safety net. The kind of move that required not just skill but faith—faith that the risk was worth it, that the pattern could be broken, that a Thorne man could choose differently just this once.

The vision shattered. He was back at the board, stones still gripped in his sweating palm. But the knowledge remained. His next move mattered, but not in the way he'd thought. Win or lose, the game was just the beginning. The real test came after, in every ordinary moment that offered a chance to choose.

Micah looked at the stones in his hand. Such small things to carry such weight. But wasn't that always the way?

"Your hands are shaking," Eldrazi observed. "Are you afraid?"

"Yes." No point in lying. The fox pressed slightly against his leg, just enough contact to remind him he wasn't alone. "I'm afraid I'm too much like them. Too weak, too selfish, too committed to comfort. What if I can't do it?"

"Then you'll know what every Thorne man before you knew—that you had a choice and chose yourself." She leaned back, shadows deepening the lines of her face until she looked older than the forest itself.

The stones grew heavy in his palm. The next move crystallized in his mind—not just for the game but for everything that came after.

Micah picked up the stones again. The safe move called to him, whispering all the reasonable reasons to protect rather than risk. But beyond it, he could see the other move—dangerous, costly, but carrying the possibility of transformation.

"One more thing," he said. "The fox. What is it?"

The creature lifted its head at the mention, eyes bright with intelligence that had nothing to do with ordinary animals.

"What do you think it is?" Eldrazi asked.

Micah met those amber eyes, saw eternity looking back. "Someone who used to be like me. Who stayed."

"Close enough." Eldrazi smiled, and for a moment she looked young, looked kind, looked like someone who'd spent centuries hoping to see what might happen next. "Make your move, Micah Thorne. Choose your path."

This was it. His moment. The choice that would determine whether he broke the pattern or proved it unbreakable.

The stones trembled in his raised hand, waiting for him to choose their path.

Waiting for him to choose his own.

Micah looked at the board, seeing past the immediate position to the deeper patterns. Eldrazi's experience showed in every move, her understanding of the game's deeper rhythms far exceeding his own.

The familiar desire to quit crept up on him like a stalking predator, like a jackal in the trees. But still, he played on.

The hourglass showed more sand above than below now. Time running short, the game demanding conclusion. Micah counted stones—Eldrazi had more, but not insurmountably more. If he could find the right sequence, if he could see the pattern that would cascade into victory...

But even as he searched for winning moves, he understood that wasn't really the point. The game had already given him what he'd come for—clarity. Understanding. The curse unraveling with each stone placed, each pattern completed. He was playing now not to win but to play well, to honor the game and the woman across from him and all the men who'd failed before him.

His next move was beautiful rather than strategic. Stones arranged in a spiral that echoed the fire pit, the clearing, the greater spiral of a bloodline winding through time toward this moment. Eldrazi's expression shifted—surprise? respect? something older and harder to name?

"Yes," she said simply, and made her own move. Not capturing, though she could have. Instead creating her own pattern, one that complemented his, that turned the board into something approaching art.

They were no longer playing against each other, Micah realized. They were playing together, creating something that transcended victory or defeat. The game itself was the point. The playing was the purpose. Win or lose had become secondary to the simple act of engaging honestly, completely, without reservation.

"My turn?" he asked, though he knew it was. His hands moved without conscious thought, selecting stones, placing them in sequence. His movements intuitive now, playing as his heart directed rather than his mind calculated.

The patterns that emerged were complex beyond planning. Spirals within spirals, mathematical relationships that spoke of fundamental forces—growth and decay, gathering and dispersal, the eternal dance of order and entropy. This was what Eldrazi had meant about the game being older than its rules.

"The sand rises," Eldrazi noted, glancing at the hourglass. "Three moves, perhaps four, before time claims its due."

Micah nodded. He could see the ending now—not who would win, that remained clouded, but the shape of completion. He made his move. She made hers. Back and forth, stones falling like rain, like stars, like all the tears the Thorne men had never shed. The board transformed with each turn, becoming something that had never existed before and would never exist again.

Then Eldrazi paused, hand hovering over the cups. "Your last move," she said. "Choose well."

CHAPTER 9:
THE BREAKING

The stones were warm in Micah's palm. Four pieces of captured night, smooth as water, heavy beyond their mass. His last real move. After this, only the counting would remain.

He had stopped calculating several turns ago. The mathematics of victory had slipped away from him somewhere in the endless exchange of stones, replaced by something older and stranger. A kind of peace, perhaps. Or acceptance. The two felt similar in the silver moonlight, indistinguishable as twins.

Eldrazi waited across the fire with the patience of mountains. Her ancient face held no triumph, no anticipation. Only that steady attention she had maintained since the game's beginning, reading not just his moves but the shape of his choosing. The crystals on her cloak caught the firelight and scattered it into flashes of starlight.

"I'm tired of running," he whispered. He hadn't meant it to be out loud, but there it was, and Eldrazi responded.

"Then stop."

He placed the first stone.

The click of obsidian on ancient wood echoed longer than it should have, rippling outward through the trees. The cup received it like a mouth accepting communion, and Micah felt something shift in the air around them.

The second stone fell into the next cup counterclockwise. Then the third. He was not just playing. He was praying, though to what or whom he could not have said. To the game itself, perhaps. To whatever force had called him here through dreams and desperation. To the possibility that a man could change, that patterns could break, that three hundred years of accumulated failure could find its end in one lost boy sitting across from eternity, choosing to see it through.

The fourth and final stone hovered over its destination for just a moment before he let it fall.

The stone clicked into place, and the board was complete.

Eldrazi studied the board for a long moment. Then she reached for her remaining stones with the fluid grace that had marked all her movements, the ease of someone who had done this exact thing more times than the forest had seasons.

Her final play was beautiful. Micah could see that even through his exhaustion, even through the strange calm that had settled over him like morning fog. She moved her stones in a cascading sequence that seemed to reorganize the entire board, each click building on the one before, the whole thing unfolding with the inevitability of tide or erosion or any other force that humans could observe but never truly control.

When she finished, her side of the board was nearly empty. Most of the stones now rested in the large cup at her end, the store where captured pieces accumulated. His own store held far fewer.

"It is done," Eldrazi said. "Shall we count?"

Micah nodded. His throat had closed around words, leaving only gesture.

They counted together, the ritual of it oddly comforting. Each stone lifted from its cup and placed carefully aside, the tally growing. Micah's store held seventeen pieces. A respectable number, especially given how badly he had been losing through the middle of the game. The visions had cost him, each revelation forcing him to play while his mind was still reeling from what he had seen.

Eldrazi's store held eighteen.

One stone. A single piece of obsidian, no bigger than his thumbnail, made the difference between winning and losing. Between walking free and joining the memorial clearing, another set of belongings carefully arranged for the next seeker to find.

Micah stared at the stone that had decided his fate. It sat among the others in Eldrazi's collection, indistinguishable, anonymous. It could have been any of them. Could have been the one he'd placed three moves ago, the one that had felt so right at the time. Could have been one of his first aggressive captures, the early greed that had set him back before he learned what the game truly wanted.

"I lost," he said. The words came out steady, which surprised him.

"Yes."

"By one stone."

"By the only margin that matters. One is enough. One is always enough." Eldrazi began gathering the stones back into their leather pouch, each piece clicking against its fellows like teeth or bones or the counting of years. "One choice. One ancestor. One moment when the hard path presented itself and the easy path was chosen instead. That is how curses are born. That is how they continue."

The fire had burned low during their counting, flames giving way to coals that pulsed with their own deep light. The clearing had grown darker, the trees leaning closer, the stars seeming brighter in compensation. The hourglass that had measured their time sat empty now, all its silver sand risen to the top in defiance of every law Micah had been taught to believe.

He should feel devastated. Should feel the weight of failure crushing him the way it had crushed every man in his line. Should be calculating how to escape, to bargain, to find some loophole that would let him walk away from the consequences of his loss.

But the feeling that filled him was something else entirely.

"I saw them," he said. "My father, my grandfather, Harold, Ezekiel. I saw what they chose and why they chose it. I felt their fear from the inside."

"Yes."

"That was the point, wasn't it? Not winning. Seeing."

Eldrazi's hands stilled on the pouch. She looked at him with those dark eyes that held too much intelligence to be merely human, and for a moment her face showed something that might have been hope. Or recognition. Or the careful attention of someone witnessing something rare and precious.

"The game measures many things," she said slowly. "Strategy, yes. Patience. The ability to think beyond the immediate move. But most of all, it measures how a player responds to what they learn about themselves. Some see their family's failures and feel only vindication. Their own weakness excused by the weakness of those who came before. Some see and feel nothing at all, the visions sliding off them like water off stone. They are the most tragic, perhaps. Offered understanding and too hollow to receive it."

"And me?"

"You wept for them. For Ezekiel's greed and Harold's desperation and your father's exhausted surrender. You saw their choices and felt compassion rather than contempt." She tied the pouch closed with a cord that looked woven from hair or grass or something older than either. "That is not nothing, Micah Thorne. That is not nothing at all."

The fox stirred, lifting its head to look at him. In the dim light of dying coals, its eyes seemed to glow with their own inner fire. There was something in that gaze that felt like acknowledgment. Like the recognition of one who had walked this path before and knew what it cost to walk it to the end.

"What happens now?" Micah asked.

He expected fear to accompany the question. Expected his body to rebel against the answer he knew was coming, against the transformation from living man to forest spirit, from seeker to warning. But the fear didn't come. What came instead was a strange lightness, as if the weight he had carried his entire life was finally, finally beginning to lift.

Eldrazi rose from her place by the fire, moving with that fluid grace that belonged to no natural creature. The crystals on her cloak caught the last light of the coals and scattered it like memory across the clearing. She was older than the trees, older than the curse, older than the family whose fate she had been appointed to judge. Yet in this moment, she looked almost sad.

"Now," she said, "we see what you have truly chosen."

With a silent grace, she wrapped her hand around his, pressing one of the smooth stones into his palm.

"You will find the stone when you need it," she said, raising her other hand up to his cheek, resting her papery flesh against his for just a moment, as the world went dark.

Micah woke with a gasp that tore itself from somewhere deeper than his lungs.

Light. Too much light. He threw his arm across his eyes, the brightness painful after so long in the forest's perpetual twilight. His other hand was clenched around something hard and familiar, something that pressed ridges into his palm with the particular insistence of objects that mattered.

His car keys.

He lowered his arm slowly, letting his eyes adjust. The light resolved itself into ordinary afternoon sun, slanting through a windshield spotted with dust and the remains of insects. Beyond the glass, trees. A gravel parking lot. A brown sign with yellow letters that he couldn't quite read from this angle but somehow knew said something about trail access and permit requirements.

He was in his car.

He was reclined in the driver's seat of his Honda, keys clutched in his right hand, body twisted awkwardly against the door as if he had fallen asleep in the middle of reaching for something. Through the windshield, the trailhead waited. The same trailhead he had driven six hours to reach. The same trailhead he had walked through into impossibility.

Hadn't he?

Micah sat up slowly, vertebrae protesting the movement. His neck ached with the particular stiffness that came from sleeping at wrong angles. His mouth tasted of staleness and he tried desperately to conjure up some saliva. The clock on the dashboard glowed green in the afternoon light: 3:47 PM.

That couldn't be right. He had arrived in the morning. Had parked, had gathered his supplies, had walked into the forest and spent days—days—wandering its impossible depths. Had played a game under stars that wheeled overhead in patterns that spoke of forces beyond human comprehension. Had made a choice that shattered a curse three centuries old.

Hadn't he?

He turned to look at the back seat. His backpack sat exactly where he had placed it before... before what? Before falling asleep? Before entering the forest? The zipper was closed. The sleeping bag was still strapped to the bottom, compression sack undisturbed. His water bottles stood in the cup holders, still full, still sealed.

His phone lay on the passenger seat, screen dark. He picked it up, pressed the power button. Nothing. Dead battery, or something worse. He remembered it dying in the forest, remembered the screen going black and staying black no matter how he tried to revive it. But that had been days ago. That had been in a place where electronics failed and time moved like honey.

Micah set the phone down and looked at his hands.

They were clean. There was no sign of the dirt acquired from gathering wood and filtering water and gripping tree bark for balance on slopes that shouldn't have existed.

He turned his hands over, examining them in the afternoon light. No scratches ran across his knuckles, the thin lines of dried blood that had plagued him for days. Gone too were the blisters.

What happened to me?

Micah pulled down the sun visor and looked at himself in the mirror.

A stranger looked back.

Not entirely a stranger. The eyes were his, brown and familiar, though they held something now that he couldn't quite name. But the face around those eyes had changed. His cheekbones stood out sharply. His jaw seemed more pronounced. He couldn't point to anything measurable that was different. And yet it was. All of it.

He touched his face, feeling the exact amount of beard growth that had been there when he arrived. If he had spent days in the forest, he'd have almost a full beard by now. But it was just a heavy case of five o'clock shadow.

The contradictions piled up like stones in his mind, each one demanding explanation that none of the others could provide. His supplies were untouched, but his face held the signs of a life-altering journey. His phone was dead, but the dashboard clock suggested only hours had passed. He was here, in the parking lot, but the evidence written in his mind said he had been somewhere else entirely.

Micah opened the car door and stepped out into the afternoon.

The air hit him first. Clean and cold and real, carrying the scent of redwoods and distant rain. He breathed it in, filling lungs that felt somehow larger than they had before, and for a moment the world swam around him. His legs were weak, unsteady, the muscles of someone who had walked for days without adequate food or rest.

He caught himself on the car door, waiting for the dizziness to pass. The gravel beneath his feet crunched with satisfying ordinariness. The trees at the edge of the parking lot stood motionless, their bark rough and brown and entirely mundane. No eyes watched from their whorls. No whispers carried on the wind.

The trailhead was thirty feet away. A wooden arch marked its beginning, the words "Shadow Grove Nature Trail" carved into a plaque that looked recently maintained. Beyond the arch, a path disappeared into the trees, ordinary and inviting, the kind of trail that families walked on Sunday afternoons.

Had he walked through that arch? Had he passed the warning sign, crossed the threshold, entered the forest that had called him through dreams and desperation?

He couldn't remember. That was the worst part. He could remember everything that came after—the fog, the fox, the memorial clearing with its carefully arranged belongings—but the actual moment of entry had dissolved into uncertainty. He might have walked in. He might have sat in his car and dreamed the whole thing, his exhausted mind creating elaborate fictions from the raw material of his research and his need.

Micah walked to the trailhead on legs that felt borrowed from someone else. The arch cast a shadow across the path, and he stopped at its edge, unwilling to cross. He wasn't afraid. Instead, he felt that whatever had happened, whatever was real or imagined, the crossing had already been made. Going back in would prove nothing. Would answer nothing. Would only muddy further what was already impossibly unclear.

He stood there for a long time, watching the shadows shift as clouds moved across the sun. The forest beyond the arch was just a forest. Trees and ferns and the filtered light of late afternoon.

A car pulled into the parking lot behind him, gravel crunching under its tires. Micah turned to watch a family unload—mother, father, two children already bouncing with the particular energy of kids who had been confined too long. The father caught his eye and nodded, the universal greeting of strangers in shared spaces.

"Trail open?" the man called.

Micah looked back at the arch, at the ordinary path disappearing into ordinary trees. "I don't know," he said honestly. "I haven't gone in."

The family gathered their supplies—small backpacks, water bottles, the youngest child clutching a stuffed animal that had clearly been a condition of the expedition. They walked past Micah with cheerful unconcern, passed beneath the arch, and disappeared into the forest without ceremony.

Nothing happened to them. No fog descended. No signs appeared bearing cryptic warnings. They were just a family on a hike, walking a trail that thousands of other families had walked before them.

Micah returned to his car.

He sat in the driver's seat for a long time, hands resting on the wheel, staring at the trailhead without really seeing it. The evidence warred within him, refusing to resolve into coherent narrative. His body said one thing. His car said another. His memory offered only fragments, pieces of a puzzle that might form a picture or might be nothing but scattered noise.

Did it matter?

The question surfaced from somewhere deep, floating up through the confusion like a bubble through dark water. Did it matter whether the forest had been real? Whether Eldrazi existed outside his exhausted imagination? Whether the fox had truly guided him or whether he had simply sat in this car and dreamed of guidance while his body ate itself from within?

Whether that change had happened in a mystical forest or in the fevered dreams of a man having a breakdown in a parking lot—did it matter? Wasn't the change itself what mattered? Wasn't the direction more important than the terrain it crossed?

Micah started the car.

The engine turned over immediately, familiar and reliable. The gas gauge showed half a tank, enough to get him home without stopping. His phone was still dead on the passenger seat, but he didn't need it. He knew the way. Had driven these roads just... hours ago? Days ago? The uncertainty no longer felt maddening. It felt almost peaceful. A mystery he could carry without needing to solve.

He pulled out of the parking lot without looking back at the trailhead. The road wound through forest for the first few miles, redwoods pressing close on either side, their trunks massive and ancient and entirely ordinary. Then the trees thinned, gave way to farmland, and the highway appeared ahead like a promise or a question.

South. Home. Back to the apartment with its stale air and its unpaid bills and its particular silence that had felt like death before he'd left.

It would feel different now. He was almost certain of it. Not because the apartment had changed but because he had. Because somewhere in the space between parking his car and starting it again, something fundamental had shifted. A choice had been made that couldn't be unmade. A pattern had begun to break that couldn't be unbroken.

Or he was delusional. Suffering from some combination of exhaustion and stress and the particular madness that came from too much time alone with dark thoughts. The sense of transformation might be nothing more than the euphoria of survival, the brain rewarding itself for not dying with a flood of neurochemicals that felt like revelation.

Both explanations felt true. Both felt false. Micah drove south through the fading afternoon, suspended between certainties, holding the contradiction without trying to resolve it.

The highway stretched ahead, empty and patient, offering no answers.

He drove for three hours before stopping for gas. The station was a small one, the kind that survived on locals and the occasional tourist who had missed the bigger exits. Micah filled his tank and went inside to use the bathroom, avoiding the mirror this time, not ready to see again how much his face had changed.

When he came out, the attendant—a woman in her sixties with gray hair pulled back in a practical ponytail—looked at him with something between concern and curiosity.

"You okay, hon? You look like you've been through it."

Micah considered the question. Through what? Through a forest that might not exist?

"Long trip," he said finally. "Longer than I expected."

She nodded, accepting this as explanation. "Well, you be careful on the road. Getting dark soon. You got far to go?"

"A few more hours."

"You want some coffee? Looks like you could use it."

He did want coffee. Wanted the ordinary ritual of it, the specific reality of hot liquid in a paper cup, something tangible to hold against the uncertainty that had become his constant companion. He paid for a large black coffee and a package of peanuts—the first food he'd purchased in... how long? The question no longer had a clear answer.

Back in the car, he ate the peanuts slowly, feeling them settle into a stomach that wasn't sure how to process the sudden arrival of actual sustenance. The coffee was bitter and perfect and entirely real. These small things anchored him, proof that whatever else was true, he still existed in a world where gas stations sold coffee and helpful strangers asked if you were okay.

The sun set as he drove, painting the western sky in shades of orange and purple that looked almost like the impossible colors of the forest's twilight. Almost, but not quite. The real sky followed rules. Obeyed physics. Transitioned smoothly from day to night without stopping to ask whether time felt like moving forward or standing still.

By the time he reached his exit, full darkness had fallen. The city rose around him, familiar and strange, its lights reflecting off low clouds that threatened rain. His apartment waited somewhere ahead, unchanged and unchanging, the place where his life before the forest would meet his life after.

If there was an after. If the forest had been real. If any of it had been more than elaborate dream and desperate hope.

CHAPTER 10:
A NEW DAWN

The first morning back, Micah woke before dawn.

This was unusual. For as long as he could remember, mornings had been enemies to be negotiated with, alarm clocks snoozed into submission, consciousness accepted only under protest. But he opened his eyes in the gray pre-light and found himself alert, present, his mind clear in a way that felt both foreign and familiar.

He lay still for a long moment, taking inventory. His body ached in ways that would make no sense if he had simply driven to a parking lot and back. The apartment surrounded him with its particular silence. Not empty silence, but full silence, weighted with all the things he had accumulated and neglected. Dishes that needed washing. Laundry that needed doing. Bills that needed paying. A life that needed living, if he could remember how.

He got up.

Such a small thing. Such an ordinary action. But it felt different now, felt deliberate in a way that getting up had never felt before. He was not rising because he had to, not dragging himself vertical through sheer momentum. He was choosing to rise. Choosing to face the day. Choosing to begin.

The kitchen was worse than he remembered. The dishes had developed a film in his absence, the particular patina of neglect that came from food left too long in standing water. He rolled up his sleeves and started washing, the hot water a small comfort against the morning chill. Each plate cleaned and set aside felt like progress. Each glass restored to transparency felt like proof that things could be made right again.

When the dishes were done, he moved to the laundry. Sorted darks from lights with the careful attention of someone learning a new skill. Measured detergent, loaded the machine, listened to the water begin its cycle. Just like his mom had taught him. These were tasks he had done a thousand times before, but never like this. Never with this sense of presence, of intention, of each small action mattering.

The bills waited on the counter where they had always waited, their envelopes soft with age and handling. Micah sat at his small table and opened them one by one, confronting the numbers that had felt so insurmountable before. The power bill was past due but not yet critical. The phone bill could be paid with what remained in his account. The rent—

The rent was a problem. Three days late already, with more days accumulating while he had wandered or dreamed. His landlord's patience was not infinite. His bank account was not bottomless. The practical realities of his life had not been transformed by mystical forest games, whether real or imagined.

But he could make a call. Could explain, apologize, negotiate. Could do the hard thing instead of avoiding it until avoidance became catastrophe. His father had avoided calls like this. His grandfather had let bills pile up until the piling became burial. The pattern was clear, and the pattern could be broken. He had already done so, and would keep doing it.

He dialed his landlord's number before he could talk himself out of it.

The conversation was exactly as unpleasant as he had anticipated. Mr. Hendricks was not sympathetic to excuses, did not care about personal crises or unexpected trips. He wanted his money, wanted it soon, wanted assurances that this would not become a pattern. Micah listened without defending himself, apologized without making excuses, promised payment by Friday and meant it.

When he hung up, his hands were shaking. The old familiar shame rose in his throat, the voice that said he was worthless, irresponsible, destined to fail at even the most basic requirements of adulthood. But beneath the shame was something else now. Something that felt almost like pride. He had made the call. Had faced the consequence. Had done the hard thing instead of hiding from it.

Such a small victory. Such an ordinary accomplishment. But it was his, and it was real, and it was the beginning of something that could become a direction if he let it.

The auto shop was next.

He found Derek's number in his call history, still there from the interview he had slept through a lifetime ago. The conversation was brief, awkward, probably pointless. Derek remembered him, remembered the missed interview, was professionally skeptical about second chances. But he took Micah's number again, said he would call if anything opened up, said it with the particular tone of someone who would probably not call but appreciated the effort.

It didn't matter. The call itself mattered. The choosing to make it instead of letting the opportunity dissolve into the long list of things Micah had failed to follow up on. Even if nothing came of it, he had acted. Had shown up, if only by phone. Had moved one small tree instead of walking around it.

The day passed in a rhythm of small tasks and smaller victories. He cleaned the bathroom, scrubbing grout with a focus that felt almost meditative. He took out the trash that had been accumulating for longer than he wanted to admit. He watered the plant on his windowsill—dead, of course, brown and brittle and beyond salvation—and then threw it away instead of leaving it to remind him of his failures.

By evening, the apartment looked different. Hardly magazine-ready, but cared for. Attended to. The space of someone who was trying, even if the trying was imperfect.

Micah sat on his couch as darkness fell outside his windows, exhausted in a way that felt earned rather than inevitable. His body was still recovering from whatever had happened to it—the weight loss, the muscle depletion, the particular fatigue that came from days without adequate food. But his mind felt clearer than it had in years. Alert. Present. Ready.

His phone had finally charged enough to turn on. He watched it boot up with the particular anxiety of someone expecting bad news, watching the notifications populate the screen one by one. Missed calls, mostly from numbers he didn't recognize. Text messages, mostly spam. And one voicemail, from a number he did recognize.

David.

The message was brief, casual, carrying none of the weight that Micah projected onto it. "Hey, cuz. Just checking in. Haven't heard from you in a while. That Thursday thing I mentioned is still happening if you're interested. Give me a call."

The timestamp was from three days ago. Before the forest. Before the game. Before everything had changed or nothing had changed, depending on which evidence you believed.

Micah listened to the message twice, three times, letting his cousin's voice wash over him. That easy confidence. That genuine care wrapped in casual words. David had called to check in, had thought of him during an ordinary week, had extended the invitation again despite Micah's previous refusals.

His thumb hovered over the callback button.

The old resistance rose immediately, familiar as breathing. Thursday nights were his. He needed his alone time. The group would be awkward, uncomfortable, full of people who had their lives together looking at him and seeing his obvious failure. Better to stay home. Better to avoid the whole thing. Better to text back something noncommittal and let the opportunity fade like all the others.

Except.

Except he had stood in a clearing under impossible stars and chosen to stop. Had felt the weight of three hundred years of easy choices and understood where they led. Had watched his father walk around trees and learned exactly what that walking cost.

He pressed the button.

David answered on the third ring, surprised pleasure evident in his voice. "Micah! Hey, man. I was starting to think you'd fallen off the earth."

"Something like that." The words came out rougher than intended, carrying more truth than he had meant to reveal. "I've been... away."

"Away? Like vacation away, or..."

"I don't know how to explain it." Micah found himself laughing, the sound unfamiliar in his own ears. "I drove north. To a forest. I think I got lost. I'm not entirely sure what happened, but I'm back now, and I'm..."

He trailed off, uncertain how to finish. Different? Changed? Possibly insane?

"You okay?" David's voice had shifted, concern replacing casualness. "You sound weird. Not bad weird, just... different."

"Yeah. Different is probably the right word." Micah took a breath, the kind that preceded jumps and confessions. "That Thursday thing. The group you mentioned. Is it too late to come this week?"

Silence on the line. Long enough that Micah wondered if the call had dropped. Then David spoke again, and his voice was careful, gentle, the voice of someone trying not to spook a skittish animal.

"It's not too late. It's never too late. We meet at seven, at the church annex facing Maple. You know the one?"

"I know it."

"Awesome. Like I said, you don't need to bring anything. Just yourself. Sound good?"

The question landed with more weight than David probably intended. Did this sound good, like something he should be doing? Like something he *could* do? Could he choose the hard thing, the uncomfortable thing, the thing that required vulnerability and effort and the admission that he couldn't fix himself alone?

"Yeah," Micah said. "I can do that."

Thursday arrived like any other Thursday, indifferent to the significance Micah had assigned it.

He changed his shirt three times, unable to decide what message he wanted to send. Too casual and he'd look like he didn't care. Too formal and he'd look like he was trying too hard. He settled on a gray henley that split the difference, hating himself for caring about something so trivial, recognizing the caring as a form of investment he hadn't felt in years.

The annex of David's church was exactly as he remembered it. It had never been his church, but every now and again, Mom and Dad would cave to David's dad and they would go on some random Sunday. After service the annex would have a table set out for donuts and coffee. Then during the week it would sometimes hold children's birthday parties and middle school dances. Brick exterior, fluorescent interior, the particular institutional smell of floor wax and old coffee. Nice, sturdy. But never a place he felt at home, only a place he visited. He parked in the lot and sat in his car for fifteen minutes, watching other people arrive.

They looked ordinary. Young, mostly, though not exclusively. Some came alone, others in pairs or small groups. They didn't look like people who had their lives together. They looked like people, carrying their own invisible weights, walking toward a building where those weights might be shared.

Micah got out of the car.

The walk from the parking lot to the front door was perhaps fifty feet. It felt longer. Each step was a choice, a small commitment that could still be reversed. He could turn around. Could drive home. Could text David an excuse and return to the familiar comfort of his empty apartment.

He kept walking.

Inside, a hallway led to a room where chairs had been arranged in a rough circle. Maybe fifteen people already seated, conversations overlapping in that particular murmur of groups forming and reforming. David saw him immediately, face breaking into a smile that held both happiness and relief.

"You made it."

"I made it."

David didn't hug him, didn't make a scene. Just gestured to an empty chair beside his own and handed Micah a paper cup of coffee that had clearly been waiting. The small kindness nearly undid him. Such a simple thing, to have someone expect you and prepare for your arrival.

He sat. The chair was metal and uncomfortable, the coffee weak and slightly burned. The room smelled of institutional heating and too many bodies in too small a space. Everything about it was imperfect, ordinary, exactly what he had expected and nothing like what he had feared.

The meeting began without ceremony. Someone named Marcus welcomed the group, invited anyone who wanted to share, reminded everyone that what was said in the room stayed in the room. Then silence, the particular silence of people deciding whether to speak.

A woman in her thirties talked about her week. A job interview that hadn't gone well. A phone call with her mother that had gone worse. The small indignities of trying to rebuild a life that had fallen apart. She spoke without self-pity, just reporting facts, and when she finished, the group murmured acknowledgment and let the silence return.

A man Micah's age shared next. Something about an ex-girlfriend, a mistake he kept making, the pattern he could see but couldn't seem to break. His voice cracked once, twice, and he apologized for it, and someone across the circle said there was nothing to apologize for.

Micah listened. Just listened. He had been afraid of being seen, of being known, of having his failures exposed to strangers who would judge him. But no one was judging. They were just... being together. Sharing weight. Doing the hard thing of honesty in a world that rewarded performance.

When his turn came—signaled by nothing more than a brief silence and a few glances in his direction—he shook his head slightly. Not ready. Not yet. The group accepted this without comment, moved on to the next person, let him be present without demanding performance.

Afterward, David walked him to his car.

"How was that?"

Micah considered the question. How was it? Uncomfortable. Awkward. Exactly as hard as he had feared. And also something else. Something that felt almost like relief. The relief of finally doing a thing you had been avoiding, of discovering that the doing was survivable even if it wasn't pleasant.

"I'll come back next week," he said.

David nodded, and there was something in his expression that looked almost like the fox's amber gaze.

"I'm glad," David said.

Micah drove home through streets that looked the same as they had always looked. The apartment waited with its cleaned surfaces and paid bills and the particular silence that no longer felt quite so much like death. He undressed, showered, lay in bed staring at the ceiling while his mind processed everything that had happened.

He still didn't know if the forest had been real. Still couldn't reconcile the evidence of his body with the evidence of his car. The uncertainty remained, a question that might never be answered, a mystery he would carry without resolution.

But he had shown up. Had sat in an uncomfortable chair and listened to strangers share their pain. Had chosen the hard thing over the easy thing, just this once, just for one Thursday evening.

Tomorrow he would have to choose again. And the day after. And the day after that. The transformation wasn't a single moment but a direction, maintained through thousands of small decisions that would never feel as significant as they were.

But tonight, he had begun.

Tonight, for the first time in years, that was enough.

Chapter 11:
Finding the Stone

Three weeks passed.

Micah marked them not by calendar days but by Thursdays. Three meetings at the church annex. Three times sitting in the uncomfortable metal chair, listening to strangers share their weight, occasionally sharing fragments of his own. Three small victories that were beginning to feel less like victories and more like habit.

The uncertainty about the forest had not faded. If anything, it had deepened, becoming part of the texture of his days. He would catch himself reaching for memories that slipped away like water through fingers—the fox's amber eyes, Eldrazi's ancient face, the particular sound of obsidian stones clicking into wooden cups. The details blurred and shifted, refusing to solidify into the kind of certainty that memory usually provided.

But the direction remained. That was what mattered. Whatever had happened in those lost days—vision or delusion, transformation or breakdown—the lessons had taken root. He was showing up. Making calls he would have avoided before. Choosing the slightly harder path when the easy one beckoned.

The job at the auto shop had come through after all. Derek had called on a Tuesday, sounding surprised by his own decision, offering a trial period that could become permanent if things worked out. The work was physical, honest, exactly what Micah needed. His hands learned the language of engines and oil, of problems that could be diagnosed and fixed, of labor that left him tired in ways that felt earned.

It was a Saturday afternoon when it happened.

Micah was doing laundry—the second load of the day, having discovered that regular maintenance was easier than crisis management. He had developed a system now, sorting clothes before they piled up, running loads on weekends when the machines in the basement were less contested.

The jacket was the one he had worn in the forest. His old hiking jacket, the one with the torn pocket and the stain that wouldn't come out. He had shoved it in the back of his closet when he returned, unable to look at it, unwilling to throw it away. But today, sorting through clothes that needed washing, he had pulled it out without thinking.

The pockets needed to be emptied before washing. Basic laundry knowledge, the kind of thing his mother had taught him years ago. He checked the left pocket first—empty. Then the right, the one with the torn lining that sometimes swallowed small objects.

His fingers closed on something smooth and cold.

For a moment, he didn't understand. His mind offered explanations—a rock picked up on some forgotten hike, a piece of broken glass worn smooth, anything that fit the shape of ordinary life. But his hand knew before his mind caught up. His hand recognized the weight, the temperature, the particular density of the thing it held.

He pulled it out.

The obsidian stone sat in his palm, catching the basement's fluorescent light and refusing to reflect it. Smooth as centuries of handling. Heavy with more than physical weight.

Micah's legs gave out.

He sat on the concrete floor of the laundry room, the jacket forgotten beside him, the washing machine humming its indifferent cycle. The stone was warm now, heated by his grip, and it fit his palm exactly as the game stones had fit. Exactly as he remembered, in the memories that kept slipping away.

It was real.

The thought arrived with the force of revelation, of conversion, of something breaking open that had been sealed too long. The forest was real. The game was real. Eldrazi and the fox and the visions and all of it—real, real, real, not fever dream or psychological crisis but something that had actually happened, something he had actually survived.

The tears came without warning.

Not the careful, controlled tears he had learned to permit himself at Thursday meetings. These were different. These were the tears of a man who had been carrying uncertainty like a stone in his chest, who had been acting on faith without knowing if faith was warranted, who had just been handed proof that his transformation was not delusion.

He wept for his father, who had never found proof, who had never known that the weight he carried could be set down. Wept for his grandfather, dying young in a foreign war, never understanding the pattern that had claimed him. Wept for Harold and Ezekiel and all the Thorne men stretching back to Salem, each one facing choices they couldn't see clearly, each one passing forward what they couldn't put down.

He wept for himself. For the years of numbness and the months of despair. For the drive north that could have ended so differently. For the grace—he could use that word now, could let it mean what it meant—that had led him to a clearing where an ancient woman waited with a game older than history.

The stone grew warmer in his grip, almost alive, pulsing with something that might have been memory or might have been presence. He could feel the forest in it. Could feel the fox's patient guidance, Eldrazi's terrible compassion, the weight of the board as he placed his final stones.

You will find the stone when you need it.

Her words, surfacing now from the blur of half-remembered visions. She had known. Had placed this anchor in his pocket or his path, had ensured that when doubt grew heavy enough to threaten his direction, proof would appear.

The stone was not evidence for a court or a congregation. No one else would ever understand what it meant, what it represented, what it had cost and what it promised. This was intimate proof. Personal confirmation. A talisman for the moments when the choosing grew hard and the old patterns whispered their familiar temptations.

Micah sat on the laundry room floor for a long time. The washing machine finished its cycle and began to beep, that insistent sound of ordinary life demanding attention. He ignored it. Let the clothes sit in their drum, growing wrinkled and damp. Some things mattered more than laundry.

Eventually, the tears subsided. The shaking in his hands stilled. He remained on the floor, back against the wall, the stone held to his chest like something precious. Which it was. The most precious thing he owned, worth more than cars or apartments or anything that could be measured in money.

That future was possible now. The curse broken.

Micah stood slowly, joints protesting the time spent on cold concrete. He transferred the clothes to the dryer, added a fabric softener sheet, and started the cycle. Ordinary actions. Ordinary life. But the stone was warm against his leg where he had slipped it into his jeans pocket, and nothing would ever be entirely ordinary again.

He climbed the stairs to his apartment, carrying laundry he would fold later and certainty he would carry forever. The sun was setting outside his windows, painting the sky in shades of amber and rose. Beautiful and temporary, like everything. Like life. Like the chance he had been given to choose differently.

He would tell no one. Would explain to no one. The stone was his alone, private as prayer, personal as the choice that had broken three hundred years of pattern.

But he would carry it always. Would touch it in moments of doubt, draw strength from its impossible weight. Would remember, when the easy path beckoned, that a woman older than memory had dealt him stones and shown him who he could become.

The curse was broken. The proof was in his pocket. And tomorrow, he would choose again.

EPILOGUE

Five years later, Micah Thorne stood in soft morning light and watched his son breathe.

The nursery was small, occupying what had been a home office in the modest house they had purchased last spring. His wife had painted the walls a pale green that reminded him of new leaves, of forests in early morning, of beginnings. A mobile of wooden animals turned slowly above the crib, casting gentle shadows that moved like living things across the sleeping face below.

The baby was three weeks old. James Michael Thorne, named for grandfathers who had never met him, who had died too young to imagine this moment. He slept with the absolute commitment of newborns, fists curled beside his head, chest rising and falling in that rhythm that still made Micah hold his own breath, counting seconds, waiting for the next small proof of life.

Such a fragile thing, a sleeping child. Such tremendous weight in such a small form.

Micah reached into his pocket and pulled out the stone.

It was warm, as it always was. Warm and smooth and heavy with more than physical mass. Five years of carrying it had not diminished its presence. If anything, it had grown more potent with time, accumulating meaning the way rivers accumulate depth. Every Thursday meeting, every hard conversation, every moment he had chosen the difficult path over the easy one, the stone had been there. Witness and reminder and proof.

He crossed to the dresser that stood beside the crib. His wife had arranged it with the particular care of new mothers, everything in its place, burp cloths folded and stacked, diapers organized by size, a small lamp that cast warm light for midnight feedings. On the wall above hung a photograph from their wedding, Micah and David standing side by side, brothers in everything but degree of blood.

There was a space on the dresser. A small clear space that seemed to have been waiting.

Micah placed the stone there, settling it gently against the wood. It looked right. Looked like it belonged. Black against pale pine, ancient against new.

"Hey."

He turned. Claire stood in the doorway, hair still mussed from sleep, wearing the robe she had owned since before they met. She was beautiful in the way that mattered, in the way that had nothing to do with morning light or careful presentation. Beautiful because she was real, present, choosing to be here with him despite knowing the weight he carried.

"Couldn't sleep?" she asked.

"Didn't want to miss this."

She crossed to stand beside him, her hand finding his with the ease of long practice. Together they looked down at their son, at the impossible fact of his existence, at the future sleeping unaware of everything that had been done to make it possible.

"The stone?" She had noticed its new placement. Of course she had.

Micah nodded. He hadn't told her everything, just that the stone reminded him to be his best every day. Even without knowing its true history, Claire knew its importance.

He still didn't know what he would tell his son about the stone, about the forest, about the curse that had hunted their family for three centuries. How do you explain to a child that his father had played a game against an ancient spirit and won—or lost, depending on how you counted—and that the winning or losing mattered less than the playing?

"He'll learn from watching you," she said. "That's how it works."

Micah thought about his father. About the watching he had done as a child, absorbing lessons that were never spoken aloud. The flinch from commitment. The turn away from difficulty. The thousand small choices that had accumulated into a pattern his father couldn't see and couldn't break.

He would be different. He already was, of course. He would never be perfect. Even with Sundays at church and Thursdays in the annex, the struggle not to return to the aimless young man he'd been remained. But every day, he persevered. He moved the tree. He picked up his cross. And that is what he would teach his son.

The baby stirred, a small sound that was not quite crying. Micah leaned over the crib and placed his hand on his son's chest, feeling the heartbeat through thin cotton. So fast, that newborn rhythm. So urgent and alive.

"I played a game once," Micah whispered, the words meant for ears too young to understand them. "In a forest that shouldn't exist, against a woman who was older than time. I lost by one stone. But losing wasn't really losing, because I played to the end. I chose to see it through."

The baby's eyes opened. Dark like his mother's, unfocused in the way of newborns, seeing shapes and light rather than the father who bent over him. But present. Aware in some fundamental way that preceded understanding.

"You won't have to play that game," Micah continued. "That's what my choosing bought you. A life without the weight I carried, without the pattern that killed your grandfathers. You get to start clean. Get to make your own choices without three hundred years of failure dragging at your heels."

Claire had moved to the window, giving him this moment. The morning light caught her profile, and Micah felt the familiar surge of gratitude that she had chosen him. That anyone had chosen him, the hollow man he had been, and stayed long enough to see who he was becoming.

He straightened, wiping his eyes with the back of his hand. The stone sat on the dresser, catching the morning light that fell through the window. It seemed to glow, just slightly, with a warmth that had nothing to do with sunshine. Eldrazi's gift. The fox's guidance. The forest's strange mercy, preserved in obsidian and memory.

His wife returned to his side. They stood together, the three of them, in the small nursery with its pale green walls and its turning mobile and its air of hope so heavy it was almost unbearable. A family. A future. A pattern broken and remade.

Micah looked at the stone one more time. Thought of the fox, wherever it was, still guiding lost souls through the forest's impossible paths. Thought of Eldrazi in her clearing, dealing games that would never end, offering chances to those brave enough or desperate enough to play.

Then he looked at his son.

"Come on," his wife said softly. "Let him sleep. There will be time."

There would be time. That was the gift. Not immortality, not freedom from struggle, but time. Years stretching ahead, each one an opportunity to choose. To show up. To be the father his father had wanted to be, to live the life his grandfathers had been denied.

Micah touched the stone one last time, feeling its warmth, its weight, its promise. Then he followed his wife out of the nursery, leaving his son to sleep beneath the turning animals, beside the stone that held three hundred years of sorrow and one man's hard-won hope.

The door closed softly behind them.

In the crib, the baby breathed.

On the dresser, the stone waited.

ABOUT THE AUTHOR

Asa Bowers writes quiet, mythic fantasy that explores the intersection of spirituality, philosophy, and the healing power of story.

He is fascinated by what different cultures consider sacred—their myths, rituals, symbols, and spiritual traditions—and how these shape the human experience.

Blending lyrical prose with psychological depth, his work draws on ancestry, folklore, and the emotional truths embedded in myth.

His debut novel, Mancala Moon, is a haunting and emotionally intimate allegory that explores the universal journey of the human soul.

***

If this book resonated with you, I would be grateful if you shared a few words in an Amazon review.

You can reach me at: abowersbook@gmail.com